Writing in books is prohibited, and all injuries to books beyond reasonable wear, and all losses, shall be promptly adjusted to the satisfaction of the librarian.

A cardholder is responsible for all books taken on his card.

Books may be kept two weeks with privilege of renewal for two weeks, excepting seven day books.

The borrower shall be subject to a fine of five cents per day for any books kept for more than two weeks, and no other books may be taken out until such fine has been paid.

SHOWDOWN AT MESILLA

Lewis B. Patten

SHOWDOWN AT MESILLA

GARDEN CITY, NEW YORK

DOUBLEDAY & COMPANY, INC.

SHOWDOWN AT MESILLA

1.

At ten o'clock on Sunday night, Si Ferguson made another run down Main Street driving his new red 1904 Maxwell with the spark retarded so that it backfired every fifty feet or so. The sounds and Sheriff Joe Chavez's disgusted curse had scarcely died away when the telephone that had recently been installed on the wall of the sheriff's office tinkled insistently.

Chavez got up out of his swivel chair and crossed to it. He put the receiver to his ear and yelled self-consciously into the mouthpiece, "Who is it and what you want?"

Chavez was a dark-skinned, stocky man of fifty-five, whose hair had all turned white. He was dressed in blue denim pants, riding boots that were scuffed and run over at the heels, and a fresh white shirt. The sheriff's badge was pinned carefully to the pocket of his shirt. His cartridge belt and holstered gun hung from a nail beside the office door so that he could get it easily as he went out.

He listened a moment, a frown deepening on his lined face. Suddenly he yelled, "Now wait a minute! Who the hell are you? What's your name and how . . ."

He held the receiver away from his ear a moment, scowling at it angrily. Then he slammed it into its cradle and turned to look at Jesse Youngbear, his deputy. "Some son-of-a-bitch that wouldn't give his name says there's a dead girl out at the Jaramillo shack. Says she's been shot."

"Want me to go out and see?"

"We'd better both go out."

"Who was it on the phone?"

"Wouldn't give his name."

"Maybe Myrtle would know who it was."

"Maybe. Go ask her."

Youngbear crossed to the phone and took the receiver down. He cranked vigorously, listened a moment and then spoke into the phone. "Myrtle, this is Jesse Young-bear. The sheriff wants to know who it was that just called here."

He listened a moment, then put the receiver back again. "She don't know, she says, but she thinks it sounded like Harvey TenEyck."

"That's who it sounded like to me but I can't be sure. He was excited and that damn contraption changes the way a voice sounds anyhow."

He took down his holstered revolver and belt. Jesse Youngbear got his from the back of his straight-backed chair and buckled it on. The two went out, closing the door behind them but not locking it.

There were arc lights at each corner all the way down Main but the rest of the town was dark except for a light burning here and there in the window of a house. Two horses were tied to the hitchrail in front of the courthouse. Chavez and Youngbear cut across the courthouse lawn, untied and mounted them.

At a walk, Chavez led the way down the street. Youngbear rode ten or twelve feet behind.

Youngbear was a tall young man, an inch over six feet in his socks. He weighed a little over two hundred pounds. His mother said he looked like his pa, who had died when he was four after being thrown from a bucking horse. His pa had been a full-blooded Sioux. His mother was a missionary on the Pine Ridge reservation when she met and married him. After his father was killed, Jesse's mother had brought him to Mesilla, and had raised him like a white.

The last arc light was in front of the depot at the lower end of Main. The two horses picked their way daintily across the tracks and then across the bridge that spanned Horse Creek. They picked up speed on the dusty road beyond.

The Jaramillo shack was off the road about a hundred yards, nestled on the bank of Horse Creek in a little grove of cottonwoods. It had been vacant a long time, but it was never locked. Chavez or Youngbear usually checked it when they rode out this way to be sure the door was shut. If it got left open a cow might wander in and accidentally close it, thus trapping herself inside where she could starve to death before anybody realized she was there.

The two dismounted in front of the shack. Chavez said softly, "Check around in back."

Youngbear walked silently into the darkness, light on his feet for so big a man. He froze when he caught movement behind the shack, relaxed almost immediately when he realized it was a tethered horse. He completed his circle of the shack and returned to the front door.

Chavez was already inside, holding a lighted match above his head. He spotted a candle on an apple box, crossed to it and lighted it.

Youngbear stared at the girl's body lying on the bed, over which a clean blanket had been thrown. He recognized her instantly. So did Sheriff Joe Chavez. He breathed a shocked, "Holy Jesus! The son-of-a-bitch wasn't lying after all."

Both men stood there a moment, recovering from their shock. Then Youngbear crossed to the girl and picked up her wrist. There was no pulse and her skin was cold. He turned his head and stared up at Chavez. "What the hell would the governor's daughter be doing in a place like this? And why would anyone . . . ?"

Chavez didn't answer, but Youngbear could tell what thoughts were going through his head by looking at his face. Chavez knew what the repercussions of this were going to be. He knew he'd better walk carefully and not make any mistakes. Chavez said, "Go back to the office and call the governor. Tell him what's happened."

He spotted something lying just under the edge of the bed and picked it up.

It was a long-barreled revolver, a Paterson Colt .36 caliber Texas Model engraved with a stagecoach holdup scene. There probably weren't a dozen such guns in the world, Youngbear thought. The only one he had ever seen belonged to King TenEyck and was kept in a velvet-lined case out at TenEyck's vast Crown ranch twenty miles south of town.

The implications of the gun's presence here struck him, coupled with the memory of what both Chavez, and Myrtle, the telephone operator had said, that the voice on the telephone had sounded like that of King TenEyck's son, Harvey. If Harvey had killed Mary Ludlow . . . hell was going to break loose for sure as soon as Governor Ludlow arrived.

Chavez said, "Go on, Jesse. Call the governor. And then you'd better call King TenEyck and tell him we've got his gun."

Jesse went out. Remembering the horse behind the shack, he stuck his head back inside. "There's a horse out back. Want me to take him in to town?"

"Yeah. Leave him at the livery. But take the saddle down to the jail."

Youngbear went around back and untied the horse. He led him to where his own horse stood.

He mounted and, leading the dead girl's horse, rode back to town. He went straight to the courthouse where he tied both horses to the rail. He unsaddled the girl's horse and carried the saddle into the jail.

He cranked for Myrtle. When she answered he said, "Get me the governor up in Denver, right away. If he's not at home, find him wherever he is. It's important. And after you've gotten me the governor, ring King TenEyck out at Crown."

He put the receiver back into its cradle, crossed the room and sat down in the sheriff's swivel chair. There was nothing to do now but wait.

He knew Harvey TenEyck had been going with Mary Ludlow. Nearly everybody in town did although he supposed it was possible that neither King TenEyck nor Governor Ludlow knew. But why would Harvey kill the girl? There had been no evidence of a struggle at the Jaramillo shack. Mary Ludlow had been fully clothed. It had looked to Jesse like she had been sitting on the edge of the bed when she'd been shot. She'd simply fallen back, probably from the force of the bullet striking her.

The phone rang and he got up and crossed the room to it. He was a little nervous now. He wasn't sure just what he ought to say to the governor. Ludlow was a resident of Mesilla and had a house up on the hill west of town. But he spent his time in Denver and had for most of the last twenty years.

Myrtle said, "I've got the governor for you, Jesse."

Jesse said, "Hello?"

The voice on the other end of the line was faint. "This is Governor Ludlow. What do you want to talk to me about?"

Jesse fairly shouted into the phone. "This is Jesse

Youngbear, the sheriff's deputy. I've got some bad news for you, I'm afraid. Your daughter . . ."

"What about my daughter? What . . . ?"

Jesse shouted, "She's been shot, Governor. Your daughter's dead."

"What? Is this some kind of joke? Who is this, anyhow?"

"I told you, Governor. This is Jesse Youngbear, the sheriff's deputy. I think you'd better get down here as fast as you can. Your daughter has been shot. I'm afraid she's dead."

"That's impossible! Let me talk to the sheriff."

"He's not here, sir. He's out at the Jaramillo shack with your daughter's body."

There was a long silence at the other end of the line. When the governor's voice came again it was hoarse and subdued. "There's a southbound train at eleven o'clock. I'll catch it, Deputy." The phone clicked and the line went dead.

Jesse hung up. He didn't suppose he had been too tactful but how do you tactfully tell a man a hundred miles away that his daughter has been murdered? He'd done the best he could.

The telephone rang again. Jesse answered it and heard the strong, arrogant voice of King TenEyck at the other end. He shouted, "This is Jesse Youngbear, the sheriff's deputy! The governor's daughter Mary has been found shot out at the Jaramillo shack! The sheriff told me to call you and tell you that a Paterson Colt like the one you have was on the floor near her body!"

He could tell that the news had shaken King TenEyck because for once the big man didn't have anything to say. He said, "Mr. TenEyck?"

"I'm here."

"Do you mind looking to see if your gun is there?"

"No. I'll look."

Jesse waited. TenEyck was gone almost five minutes. When he came back, his voice was lifeless, the way the governor's voice had been. "It's gone."

"Maybe you'd better come into town, Mr. TenEyck. The sheriff thought the voice that reported her death sounded like your son's."

"All right. I'll come." There was a click on the line.

Jesse stood staring at the phone for several minutes after he hung up. The sheriff hadn't wanted to have the phone installed, but it had certainly proved how valuable it could be tonight.

He wondered if Harvey TenEyck had killed Mary Ludlow, and if he had, wondered why. The two had apparently been seeing each other quite a lot, whenever Mary could slip away from her mother and whenever Harvey could get into town.

Jesse had always felt sorry for Harvey TenEyck. It must be hard to have a father like King TenEyck. It must be hard always trying to measure up to such a giant of a man.

TenEyck's Crown ranch was fifty miles long and twenty wide. It contained a thousand square miles of grass and timber and hay land and it supported seventy thousand cattle and nearly a thousand horses. It was worth millions. It gave TenEyck a lot of political power in the state.

TenEyck himself was a veritable giant of a man with a chest like a bull and arms as thick as the average man's thighs. He could do anything. He could break horses, rope and brand cattle, help a heifer have her first calf. He could cut timber, skid logs, run a sawmill, of which there were several on Crown. And sometimes he did these things just to prove, perhaps, that he still could though mostly he rode back and forth across Crown's vast reaches supervising his more than a hundred and fifty employees.

Jesse left the sheriff's office and untied his own and the dead girl's horse from the rail out front. He rode down the deserted street to the livery stable and led the girl's horse inside. The hostler was apparently asleep, so Jesse put the horse in a stall, taking off the bridle and replacing it with a halter.

Riding back toward the courthouse, he was thinking of the hatred that existed between TenEyck and the governor. He knew its cause and so did everybody else.

Twenty years ago, King TenEyck had stolen Ludlow's wife. At the time, Ludlow had been a state senator, politically ambitious and, like now, spending most of his time at the capital city of Denver. His wife, lonely and neglected, hadn't been able to resist the attentions of a man like King TenEyck. She became pregnant with TenEyck's child.

Though she still was Ludlow's wife, TenEyck took her out to Crown, where she bore Harvey six months afterward. And as soon as Ludlow divorced her, TenEyck married her.

She hadn't lived very long after that. People said she died from shame and remorse. She hadn't once come to town after she had moved out to TenEyck's ranch.

TenEyck raised the boy, who was pale and thin and scared. But Jesse guessed that even a boy who is pale and thin and scared longs to be a man. Harvey TenEyck had been trying to be a man for a long, long time. In his father's shadow, it wasn't an easy thing to do.

2.

The sheriff hadn't given his deputy any instructions except to call Governor Ludlow and King TenEyck, but Youngbear knew Chavez would want Mary Ludlow's body decently laid out at the undertaker's when the governor arrived. Chavez probably wouldn't notify the girl's mother. He'd let the governor take care of that.

And he would want photographs of the cabin and of the girl's body lying on the bed. Youngbear went into the office and picked up the phone. "Myrtle, get me Erasmus Cox."

He heard the phone ring at the other end of the line. It rang six times before Cox's voice answered sleepily. Youngbear said, "Ras, the sheriff's down at the Jaramillo place with a body. I figure he wants pictures of it. Can you get down there right away?"

The sleepiness went out of Cox's voice. "Right away, Jesse. I'll be there in twenty minutes."

Youngbear waited until Myrtle came back on the line. "Get me Mr. Phinney at his house."

The phone rang interminably before it was finally answered by Phinney's wife. Youngbear said, "Mrs. Phinney, this is Jesse Youngbear. There's a body at the Jaramillo place. Would you have Mr. Phinney go out and pick it up?"

"Who . . . ?"

"I can't tell you who it is, Mrs. Phinney. The sheriff will release the name." He knew if he told Mrs. Phinney that Mary Ludlow had been killed it would be all over town before Albert Phinney could even get back with her body.

She started to protest, so he cut her off by putting the phone receiver back on its hook. Since there was no longer any reason for him to remain here at the courthouse he went out, crossed the lawn, and mounted his horse. He rode down the street, heading for the Jaramillo shack.

The sheriff was sitting on the apple box out in front when he arrived. Jesse said, "The governor's coming and so is King TenEyck. I called Mr. Phinney and Erasmus Cox. I figured you'd want some pictures before you let the body be moved."

"Anybody else know?"

"Huh-uh. I didn't tell Mrs. Phinney who it was."

"Good. You stay here and wait for Cox and Phinney. I'm going to look around for Harvey. Maybe I can grab him before he gets back to TenEyck's ranch."

"Yes, sir." Youngbear sat down on the apple box as soon as the sheriff had vacated it. The sheriff untied and mounted his horse and rode back toward town.

Erasmus Cox was the first to arrive, driving his buggy. He clipped the tether weight to the horse's bridle and dug his heavy camera equipment out. He crossed the yard to the cabin door. "Who is it, Jesse?"

"Mary Ludlow. But the sheriff don't want that to get out until after the governor arrives."

"Jesus!" Cox said in an awed voice. "Who'd want to kill a nice girl like her?"

Youngbear didn't try to answer that. He said, "Get your pictures, Ras. Mr. Phinney is on his way down here with the hearse."

Cox carried his camera inside. The candle was still burning on a shelf where Chavez had put it when he brought the apple box outside. In this faint light, Cox set up his cameras. He said, "I'll get two or three shots from different angles. You figure that will be all right?"

"Sure." He supposed the sheriff had taken the gun back to town with him. Chavez probably didn't want it in the picture and its presence wasn't necessary. Both he and the sheriff had seen it on the floor beside the bed. They could testify to that.

Cox's flash went off four times. He came outside again. "I'll have the pictures for you by noon."

"That'll be fine. And no talk."

"Huh-uh." Cox picked up the tether weight, climbed into his buggy and drove away.

Albert Phinney arrived ten minutes later, driving the hearse. It was the horse-drawn hearse that Phinney'd had for years. He was trying to buy a motor-driven one but he hadn't done it yet.

Phinney, besides being the undertaker, was the county coroner. At the cabin door he asked, "Who is it, Jesse?"

"Mary Ludlow. She's been shot."

Phinney whistled. "Any idea who shot her?"

"Not yet," Youngbear lied.

"Has the governor been notified?"

"He's on the train."

"How about his wife?"

"I guess the sheriff figured it would be easier on her if we let the governor tell her Mary's dead. So if you can keep it quiet until morning . . ."

It was a hint to Phinney to keep his wife from spending the night gossiping on the telephone. Phinney understood and said, "I won't be getting home for several hours. Help me carry the body out."

"When will you have the inquest?"

"Probably day after tomorrow. But I'll have my report on the cause of death first thing in the morning."

Jesse said, "She's been shot."

"I know, but you'll need a formal report."

Youngbear helped Phinney lift the girl's body and carry it out to the hearse. She was light and easily carried and he thought what a waste it was for a pretty girl like Mary to die so young, and so violently.

Phinney closed the doors of the hearse, went around and climbed up on the seat. Jesse returned to the cabin. He folded the bloodstained blanket and tucked it beneath his arm. He blew out the candle, went out and closed the door behind him.

He untied and mounted his horse. He rode slowly and

thoughtfully back toward town, wondering where the sheriff was and what luck he'd had locating Harvey TenEyck.

Governor Ludlow would be arriving around two in' the morning. That was when the train usually went through Mesilla. It didn't stop, unless, like tonight, it carried a passenger who wanted to get off here. The mailbags were just tossed out on the platform as the train passed through.

King TenEyck might arrive an hour or so before the governor. That would give him time to locate his son and get him back to Crown. Maybe it wasn't fair but what Governor Ludlow would do to Harvey TenEyck if he got his hands on him wouldn't be fair either. Ludlow had a corps of uniformed hardcases that he called the State Police. They answered only to him and were more his personal bodyguard than they were police. He'd probably bring half a dozen of them along with him. He seldom went anywhere without that many to accompany him.

There was a light in the sheriff's office in the courthouse basement. Youngbear tied his horse, crossed the lawn and went inside. Chavez was standing in the middle of the room, scowling, a cigar clamped between his strong, yellow teeth. Jesse asked, "Find him?"

Chavez shook his head. "Damned if I know where to look. You got any ideas?"

Youngbear nodded. "One. Want me to check it out?"

"Uh-huh. Go ahead."

Youngbear went out. It was early June and the

air was crisp. There was a smoky, damp, and chilly smell in the air.

• Harvey TenEyck didn't have many friends. He had no men friends as far as Youngbear knew. He only had one other woman friend besides Mary. That was Daisy Kyle.

Daisy worked in the Cowboy's Rest Saloon. She lived in a small cabin five miles outside of town on the road to Crown. Her father, who was crippled from a railroad accident, lived with her and she provided their support, except for a pension of eight dollars a month that he got from the railroad.

Harvey TenEyck had gone with Daisy for a while before he began going with Mary Ludlow. Scared and needing help, he'd probably go to Daisy now because there wasn't any place else that he could go. Except to Crown.

Youngbear rode south, glancing at the dark Jaramillo cabin as he rode past. He suddenly wished he'd asked Chavez what he should do in case he did find Harvey TenEyck. He supposed Chavez wanted Harvey arrested and brought back to town.

That was the right thing to do, the proper thing. Yet he knew Harvey wouldn't be safe in the county jail if Governor Ludlow brought his State Police to town and decided he wanted to deal with Harvey TenEyck himself. Knowing the governor and knowing his bitter, fanatical hatred of King TenEyck, Youngbear admitted it was possible Ludlow would try to get Harvey out and hang him himself.

Alternately trotting and walking his horse, he reached

the Kyle place after midnight. There was a light in the kitchen window, a light that went out as he rode into the yard.

Harvey was here, all right, he thought. He yelled, "Daisy? This is Jesse Youngbear. Have you got Harvey TenEyck in there?"

He heard the door open. He wondered if Harvey would shoot at him and slid from his horse, taking cover behind the animal.

Daisy called, "What do you want with him?"

"I want to talk to him."

"Why?"

Youngbear was silent a moment. At last he called, "Come on, Daisy, you know why I'm here. Let's quit playing games. Light the lamp and if you've got a gun, put it away. I'm not the governor. I'm only the sheriff's deputy."

There was silence at the cabin for several minutes. They were apparently talking it over, Youngbear thought. At last he saw a match flare and a moment later saw the glow of the coal-oil lamp. Leading his horse, he walked toward the house.

He tied the animal and went to the kitchen door. TenEyck's horse was not visible. Probably tied out back to the corral fence, he thought.

Daisy stepped away from the door to let him come in. Harvey TenEyck, pale and trembling, stood in the middle of the room. Daisy's father, Jake, sat in a rocker, a blanket across his useless legs.

Youngbear said, "Harvey, I've got to take you back."

TenEyck asked with clumsily feigned innocence, "What for?"

"You know what for. For killing Mary Ludlow."

Harvey began to shake even more violently. His skin was almost gray. Even so, he was sweating heavily. Youngbear asked, "Why'd you do it, Harvey? Why Mary?"

Harvey sat down and buried his face in his hands. He sobbed uncontrollably. Youngbear frowned. He was embarrassed, for Harvey and for himself. He looked helplessly at Daisy Kyle. She said softly, "It was a suicide pact. When it came time to shoot himself, Harvey lost his nerve."

"For God's sake why? Why a suicide pact in the first place?"

There were suddenly tears in Daisy's eyes. "They were in love and they knew neither of their fathers would put up with it."

Youngbear stared at Harvey TenEyck. He couldn't help feeling a kind of angry contempt. But he felt pity too, in spite of himself. Life hadn't been easy for Harvey TenEyck. He'd felt inferior as long as he'd been able to feel anything.

But that wasn't Youngbear's problem. He was supposed to arrest Harvey TenEyck and bring him back to town. He said, "I'm sorry, Harvey, but I've got to arrest you and take you back to town."

3.

There was a long silence in the room, broken only by the tearing sounds of Harvey's sobbing. When that stopped and TenEyck looked up, Jesse could see the awful shame and guilt in the young man's eyes, which could not meet his squarely no matter how they tried.

He said, "Come on, Harvey."

"My father . . . is he in town? Does he know?"

"He knows Mary's dead and he knows his gun was on the floor beside her body. He's on his way. So's the governor."

"Do I *have* to see them?"

Jesse nodded. "I'm afraid you do. I don't know how you're going to get out of it."

Harvey threw a beseeching glance at Daisy Kyle and immediately looked down at the floor again. Jesse said, "Let's go. Is your horse tied out in back?"

Harvey TenEyck got to his feet. He started toward the door. Jesse Youngbear started after him. Behind him, he suddenly heard Daisy's trembling voice, "Jesse.

I've got a gun. You let him go." He heard the click of a gunhammer coming back.

He turned his head. Daisy had a double-barreled shotgun in her hands, pointing it at him. She was shaking and the gun muzzle was waving erratically.

Jake Kyle said angrily, "Daisy. Put that goddam thing down! It's got shells in it!"

Youngbear stopped and stood frozen, motionless, hardly daring to breathe. Very softly he said, "Daisy, don't be a fool. Put down the gun."

"Harvey, get going! I'll keep him here long enough to give you a start."

Harvey TenEyck turned his head. He stood in the doorway a moment, looking at Youngbear.

Youngbear didn't think he was afraid of going to jail, or afraid of the law, or even of Governor Ludlow. But he *was* afraid of King TenEyck. Harvey glanced beyond Youngbear at Daisy and nodded mutely. Then he turned and disappeared into the darkness outside the door.

Youngbear turned his head. "Don't do it, Daisy. Let me go after him. There's no place he can go."

"And I suppose there will be if you take him back to town?"

"He'll be safer in jail than he will be running loose."

"With the governor coming in on the train tonight?" Her voice was bitter.

"Ludlow wouldn't try to take him out of jail."

Daisy said, "You know better than that, Jesse Youngbear."

He nodded, still very conscious of the shotgun aimed at him. "All right. Maybe he wouldn't be very safe in jail. But he'd be safe enough for tonight. And tomorrow the sheriff could send him up to the state prison at Canon City."

"He wouldn't be any safer there. The warden would give him to the governor any time he asked."

Jesse didn't argue with her because he knew what she said was true. Harvey TenEyck wasn't going to be safe anywhere.

He asked, "Daisy, can I sit down?"

"All right, but don't you try anything."

He reached for a chair and straddled it, facing her, resting his arms on its back. "I can't catch him now, Daisy. I wish you'd put that thing down. It might go off."

She lowered the muzzle. "I'm sorry, Jesse. I don't want to hurt anybody. Especially not you. I just couldn't let you take that poor scared boy to jail."

"That poor scared boy killed Mary Ludlow."

"But not because . . ." Tears appeared in her eyes.

"He's got to answer for it. I've got to see he does."

"You've got to catch him first. And even if you are half-Indian you can't trail him in the dark."

The gun muzzle was now pointing at the floor. Daisy was still shaking, but her finger was no longer curled over the trigger.

She was a diminutive girl, barely over five feet tall, but she was pretty and she had a nice, easygoing way about her. Youngbear said, "Daisy, let me have the gun."

She nodded listlessly. He got up and took the gun carefully from her. He eased the hammer down, then broke the action and extracted the shells.

Daisy said, "I suppose you want to arrest me now."

"No. I don't think the sheriff will want to charge you with anything." He went to the door, after laying the shotgun on the table, the shells beside it. His hands were shaking slightly. The gun in Daisy's hands had scared him. A gun in the hands of anyone who wasn't used to guns always scared him, particularly when they were aimed at him.

He untied his horse and mounted, wondering what Harvey TenEyck was going to do. There was no place he would be safe, no place but out at Crown. And he apparently had no intention of going there.

He reached town about one in the morning. There was a buckboard tied at the courthouse rail. The team was lathered and still heaving. Jesse tied his own horse, crossed the lawn and went into the sheriff's office on the ground floor.

King TenEyck was there. So was his foreman, Dan Malloy. TenEyck's presence seemed to fill the room. He was no taller than Jesse Youngbear, but he was thicker and heavier. His gray hair was like a lion's mane. He had the Paterson Colt revolver in his hand and was looking at it. Chavez asked, "Yours?"

"You know it is."

"Any ideas how it got out at the Jaramillo shack?"

TenEyck scowled. "Christ, there are a thousand ways it could have gotten there. I've got a hundred and fifty men working for me. Any one of them could have gone into the house and stolen it."

He turned and saw Jesse. Chavez asked, "Find him?"

Youngbear nodded. "He was out at the Kyle place."

"Why didn't you bring him back with you?"

"Daisy put a shotgun on me. Harvey got away in the dark."

Chavez cursed. Youngbear said defensively, "That gun was loaded and she had the hammer back. If you'd seen the way she was shaking, you'd have held still too."

Chavez grunted, "I suppose I would."

King TenEyck asked, "Which way did he go?"

Youngbear glanced at him. "How the hell do I know which way he went? It was dark and with all the tracks around that house . . . Well, I didn't even try to find his trail."

"He'll go back to Crown."

Youngbear looked King TenEyck squarely in the eyes. "He will like hell. He'll go anyplace else, but he won't go back to Crown."

"What are you talking about?"

"He's worse afraid of you than he is of either the law or the governor."

"He is like hell! Besides, I don't care if the gun was there, Harvey didn't kill that girl."

"Yes he did. It was a pact. He was to kill her and then kill himself. He lost his nerve when it came time to kill himself."

"That's a lie!"

"It's no lie."

"Harvey didn't say that, did he?"

"No. But Daisy did. And Harvey didn't say other-wise."

TenEyck turned to Dan Malloy, stocky, short, hard-faced, and competent. "Turn out the crew. Every damn one of them. I want Harvey found. I want him brought home to Crown."

"Yes sir."

"And make it fast. Take the buckboard to the livery. Get a fresh horse there. That goddam Ludlow will be here on the train in less than an hour. You can bet he'll have his thugs with him."

"All right." Malloy hurried out. A few moments later Youngbear heard the buckboard rattle away down the street.

TenEyck shoved the gun into his belt. Chavez said, "Leave that gun here, Mr. TenEyck. It's evidence."

"It's mine. I'll take it with me if you don't mind."

Youngbear said, "He minds. Leave the gun."

"You damn half-breed . . . !"

"Put the gun on the desk, Mr. TenEyck."

"And if I don't?"

"You will."

TenEyck stared at Youngbear and Youngbear stared back at him. He didn't know if the gun was loaded or not but he supposed it was. He didn't know if TenEyck would try to use it or not. What he did know was that if he and the sheriff let TenEyck bully them now they'd both just as well resign.

TenEyck's face was red and his eyes were like gray bullets in the cylinder of a gun. Slowly he withdrew the Paterson Colt. He extended it to Youngbear, holding it by the barrel as he did. Youngbear took it, crossed the room and laid it on the sheriff's desk.

TenEyck headed toward the door. Joe Chavez said, "Mr. TenEyck."

TenEyck turned. "What?" He was scowling but there was something in the depths of his eyes . . . It couldn't have been fear, Jesse thought, but neither was it arrogance.

The sheriff said, "I don't want your men clashing with those of the governor."

TenEyck didn't reply. He stared at Chavez a moment, shifted his glance briefly to Youngbear, then turned his head and stalked out the door. He slammed it behind him so hard that Youngbear thought the glass was going to break.

Youngbear went to the door, opened it and stepped outside. He could see King TenEyck's bulky figure striding swiftly down the deserted street in the direction of the livery barn.

The man turned suddenly and came striding back. He said, "I forgot about the goddam telephone."

Youngbear stood aside and TenEyck came in. The big man looked at Chavez. "Can I use your telephone?"

"Sure. Help yourself."

TenEyck took down the receiver and cranked vigorously. He shouted, "This is King TenEyck! I want you to ring my telephone out at my ranch!"

He waited for a long time. Youngbear thought that probably everybody out at Crown was asleep. At last somebody answered the phone and TenEyck yelled, "Malloy is on his way out there. I want you to go out to the bunkhouse and rouse the men. They're to gather up everybody they can find and have 'em there at the house by the time Malloy arrives. Malloy will tell 'em what to do."

He slammed the receiver back onto its hook. Without saying anything but a brief, "Thanks," he went outside again.

Chavez said, "Whew!"

Youngbear grinned. "What do we do now?"

"Try to keep 'em apart, I suppose. Why the hell couldn't Harvey have taken up with some other girl? Why did it have to be the daughter of the governor?"

Youngbear shrugged.

"Any idea where Harvey might go now?"

Youngbear shook his head. "He'll probably just wander around. There's no place he *can* go. He hasn't got any friends that I know of."

"King TenEyck will go out to Daisy's place and pick up his trail as soon as it gets light."

Youngbear crossed the room to the office stove. He shook down the ashes, put in some wadded-up newspaper and some kindling wood. He lighted it, closed the door and shook the coffeepot to see if any coffee was left in it. He said, "It's going to be a damn long night."

"Uh-huh." Chavez was frowning worriedly. "How in the hell are we going to keep those two apart?"

Youngbear didn't bother trying to answer him. Chavez didn't expect an answer anyway. The stove began to roar and a few minutes later the coffeepot began to sing as it heated. When it began to boil, Youngbear got two cups and poured them full. He took the sheriff one of them.

The town was silent. No one was in the cells down the corridor. It was Sunday night and the saloons were closed. Apparently Si Ferguson had driven his Maxwell home after that last pass down Main Street.

Youngbear caught himself listening for the train, even though he knew it wasn't due.

Usually he liked the sound of the train whistling as it neared the outskirts of the town. It had a far-away, mournful sound that made Youngbear think of distant places that he'd never seen.

But this morning the whistle of the train would only be a signal that trouble was descending on the town. When the governor and his State Police stepped off the train, hell was going to break loose. Nothing anyone could do would change that fact.

4.

The distant train whistle rolled mournfully across the town half an hour before its usual time and Youngbear knew the governor had been able to persuade the engineer to speed up the train as a personal favor to him.

Joe Chavez got up out of his squeaky swivel chair. He crammed his hat down tight over his white hair and grunted at his deputy, "Let's go down to the station and meet the train. The governor will expect it and anyway, we'd just as well get it over with."

Youngbear turned off the light and followed him out the door. They untied their horses, mounted, and rode unhurriedly down the street. Both could now hear the puffing of the train in the still, predawn air.

Youngbear realized that the muscles in his arms and legs were tense. They were as tense as if he was going to the station to try and capture a criminal.

At the edge of town the train whistled again and a few moments later it came puffing into the station. The engine went past, positioning the Pullman in front of the station door.

A conductor swung down and placed the portable steps on the platform. Sam Rork, chief of the governor's State Police was the first to alight. He was a trim, muscular man in a tailored blue uniform and wide-brimmed, blue felt hat. Light from the station windows reflected from the ornate gold badge he wore on the pocket of his shirt. A pearl-handled Colt's .45 revolver hung holstered at his side. He saw both Chavez and Youngbear but for the moment he chose to ignore their presence. Chavez muttered to himself, "The biggety son-of-a-bitch!"

The governor stepped onto the platform next. He was followed by eight more state policemen, scrambling in their haste. They immediately formed a protective semicircle around the governor, as if there might be some unknown threat to his safety here.

Governor Ludlow's blue serge suit had a knife-edge crease in the trousers despite the hour, despite his long train ride. He wore a white shirt and a blue and cream striped necktie. He wore cream-colored gaiters over his black shoes.

He stood tall and erect as he stared at Chavez and Youngbear across the platform. Stubbornly, Chavez waited for the governor to come to him.

Frowning slightly, Ludlow did. Handsome with his graying hair and flowing mustache, he extended a hand to Chavez. "Good to see you, Joe. Thanks for having your deputy call me."

"You're welcome, sir. I'm sorry about . . ."

Ludlow interrupted him. "Does Mrs. Ludlow know?"

"No sir. I thought you'd prefer to tell her yourself. She was probably asleep when I got the news anyway. I . . ."

Ludlow never let anybody finish a sentence if he could help it. Now he interrupted, "Where is my daughter's body?"

"At Mr. Phinney's, sir."

"Have you got the man who killed her, Joe?" Governor Ludlow liked to call people by their first names. He thought it made him seem more friendly, thought it put him on their level and since he needed their votes, that was where he wished to be. The trouble was that most times it sounded like he was patronizing them.

"Not yet, Governor."

Ludlow frowned. "Have you got any leads?"

"Well . . ."

Ludlow's voice was sharp. "Don't keep anything from me, Joe. If you know anything, I have a right to know it too."

"Well, we found a gun beside the body. It's likely the one that was used to kill her, sir."

"What kind of gun?"

"A Paterson Colt."

"A Paterson Colt? Why that's an antique gun."

"Yes sir."

Sam Rork, who had once worked at Crown interrupted now. "King TenEyck's got a gun like that."

The governor's face darkened. Behind him the train puffed as it began to move out of the station, the puffs coming closer together as it picked up speed. Ludlow asked, "Was it TenEyck's gun?"

"Yes, sir. He identified it as his."

"It was that boy of his, wasn't it?" The governor's eyes were glittering now. His mouth was drawn out into a thin and angry line.

The sheriff said resignedly, "I think it probably was, although we don't know for sure."

"Why would he kill Mary, for God's sake? They didn't even know each other."

Chavez said, "They knew each other, sir. They been going together for quite a while."

"Why didn't you tell me that before this happened? By God . . ."

Chavez said angrily, "It ain't my business to keep tabs on your family, Governor."

Rork said evenly, "Watch it, Chavez. Don't get smart with the governor."

Chavez swung his head. "And don't you get smart with me. This is my county and you've got no authority here. Remember it."

Governor Ludlow's eyes were still glittering. Youngbear could see the veins in his forehead standing out. But his voice was placating even though it had a tightly menacing quality. "Gentlemen! Quarreling isn't going to get us anywhere. Besides, I want to see my daughter. And when I have done that I want to see my wife."

At this hour no rigs were available. Ludlow stepped

down off the platform and started up the street. Rork walked beside him and the State Policemen walked in a group behind. They made a small procession as they marched up the exact middle of the street, like a parade. Phinney's Funeral Parlor and Furniture Store was three blocks away. The governor and his entourage disappeared almost at once into the darkness, only to reappear moments later beneath the first arc light.

Chavez cursed softly beneath his breath. He said, "I was thinkin' about retiring before the last election, Jesse. I was going out to my ranch and sit in a rocker on the porch. Now I wish I had."

Youngbear wondered where King TenEyck was. He was probably still in town, waiting for Malloy to return with the crew. Youngbear hoped he'd have sense enough to stay clear of the governor. King TenEyck was a big man but tonight he was alone. Governor Ludlow had nine men with him, any one of which would kill unhesitatingly if he ordered it.

He untied his horse, mounted, and followed Chavez up the street. He saw the lights go on in Phinney's store and saw the square of light as the street door opened to admit the governor and his men.

Youngbear felt sorry for Harvey TenEyck. He felt sorry for Mary Ludlow, too. But he couldn't find it in himself to feel sorry for the governor. Nor could he pity King TenEyck. Both were ruthless, overbearing men whose ambition had led them to completely neglect their families. Governor Ludlow hadn't seen Mary more than twice last year. TenEyck had bullied Harvey until his son was nothing but a shell. Harvey hadn't even had the courage to complete the pact he'd made with Mary by shooting himself after he shot her.

But pity wasn't what was going to be required of Sheriff Chavez and Deputy Youngbear in the coming days. They'd have their hands full trying to keep the peace.

As they halted at the courthouse tie rail, Chavez said, "Come on in, Jesse, and make a fresh pot of coffee. When something happens, we won't have no trouble hearing it."

Youngbear followed the sheriff into the office. Chavez turned on a light and as soon as he had, Jesse built up the fire, which had died to a bed of coals. He rinsed out the coffeepot, refilled it at the sink, then put it on the stove. He got the coffee and put some into the pot.

He suddenly was tired and realized that neither he nor the sheriff had gotten any sleep. He said, "Why don't you go home and go to bed? I'll keep an eye on things. I don't think anything's going to happen tonight."

Chavez hesitated, finally nodding and getting up out of his chair. He put on his hat and went out the door, saying as he did, "See you around noon. You can sleep in one of the cells."

Jesse sat down in the sheriff's swivel chair and put his booted feet up on the sheriff's desk. The fire roared in the stove and the coffeepot made a singing sound as it heated. He stared at the door, realizing that he was listening.

For the sound of trouble in the streets. For the sound of gunshots. For the sound of two giants clashing in a battle long postponed.

Governor Ludlow stared down at the pale face of his daughter Mary. She was lying in a casket in Phinney's Funeral Parlor situated at the rear of the furniture showroom. There was a white satin pillow beneath her head. Her expression was peaceful. There was no hint of terror or fear in it, and Ludlow wondered fleetingly what she had been thinking as she died.

He shook himself visibly and turned away. He had to go home. He had to tell his wife that Mary was dead, murdered, and he knew it was not going to be an easy thing to do.

He went out into the street. The eastern horizon was already gray.

He saw a figure standing on the sidewalk down in front of the Elkhorn Hotel and recognized it instantly as that of King TenEyck. He turned his head and spoke to Rork. "There's TenEyck now. Keep an eye on him and if he leaves town, follow him. You'd better get some horses for yourself and your men down at the livery barn. I'm going home."

"Yes, sir." Rork raised a hand to his hat in a kind of relaxed salute.

Ludlow said, "Don't tangle with TenEyck if you can help it. But I want that boy." There was implacable determination in his voice.

"Yes, sir." Rork watched the governor walk west

toward his house on the hill at the edge of town. There was a slump in Ludlow's normally straight shoulders. The long night and the sight of his daughter's dead body had taken its toll of the man, Rork thought, despite the way he seemed to have held up under it.

He turned his head. "Simms, go after the governor. Keep an eye on things up there."

"Yes, sir." Simms hurried away in the direction Governor Ludlow had gone. Rork said, "The rest of you come with me. We'd better get some horses. We'll need them if TenEyck takes a notion to leave town."

He walked down Main toward the livery stable at its lower end. The sky was lighter now, a dingy gray that cast a light of sorts into the streets.

They passed the Elkhorn Hotel. King TenEyck stared at them as they went past. It was too dark to tell what his expression was and he didn't speak.

No one was at the livery. Rork said, "Find horses for yourselves and saddle up."

The men scattered among the stalls. Ten minutes later the last of them led his saddled horse into the street. Rork said, "Jorgensen, keep an eye on King Ten-Ecyk. We'll be over at the restaurant."

A light was burning in the restaurant half a block above the depot. Rork rode to it, dismounted, and tied his horse. The others followed him inside.

They all sat down at the counter. A sleepy-looking, dark-skinned man came from the kitchen. He said sourly, "Coffee ain't even made. You'll have to wait."

Rork said, "We'll wait. But make it as quick as you

can." From where he sat, he could see the front of the Elkhorn Hotel. He could see King TenEyck waiting there.

Rork had once worked for King TenEyck and he thought he knew the man pretty well. TenEyck wasn't going to give his son up to the law.

He wished Governor Ludlow had brought along more men. King TenEyck had a hundred and fifty working for him. Nine men against a hundred and fifty wasn't very good odds no matter how you looked at it.

He remembered the implacable determination that had been in Governor Ludlow's eyes. He made himself relax but he didn't take his eyes off the powerful figure of King TenEyck standing in front of the hotel.

5.

The governor walked up the hill wearily. It had been a long day. He'd not been able to sleep coming down here on the train. He'd been too upset. But he wasn't a young man any more and a night without sleep got to him quicker than almost anything.

He reached the house. He had a key and used it. He didn't see Simms following him.

Inside the house, he groped for the light switch, found it and turned on the electric light in the hall.

The carpeting was red, the furniture dark as ebony, upholstered in red and gold. He called up the stairs, "Emmy? It's me. Get up and put on your robe. I want to talk to you."

He heard her querulous voice and he called again, "It's me. Put on your robe and come downstairs. I want to talk to you."

He heard the floor creak upstairs as she got out of bed. He followed her progress along the hall and down the stairs by the creaking floorboards, thinking irritably,

By God, when you pay as much as we did for this house, the floor hadn't ought to squeak. But the floor had creaked when they bought the house and all the time they'd owned it and anyway, he never noticed it unless he was upset.

Emmy's sallow face was lined with the years. Her gray hair was contained in a gingham cap with elastic around the bottom to hold it in place. She wore a shapeless print flannel nightgown and slippers. She said, "Robert! What in the world brings you home in the middle of the night? I thought you were in Denver."

"I was. I got a call from the sheriff a little before midnight. Come in and sit down, Emmy. I've got to talk to you."

They did not kiss, not even a dutiful peck. He looked at her coldly, with some distaste. Women aged faster than men, he thought. The years didn't sit as well on them as they did on a man. She asked, "What is it? Can't it wait until morning?"

For some reason, her question irritated him. He said coldly, "No, it can't wait. Mary's dead." He knew he had put it brutally but he didn't care. He was wondering where the affection he had once felt for this woman had gone. When had it disappeared? Had it evaporated suddenly or had he lost a little of it every day until there was nothing left?

Her face had gone dead white. There was something stricken in her eyes. They pleaded silently with him to tell her he wasn't serious. He repeated, "Mary's dead. I just identified her body down at Phinney's."

She shook her head dumbly. She got up and went into the hall. She looked upstairs and called shrilly, "Mary? Mary, you come here! Come down here this instant! Your father's . . ." She stopped, then screamed the word forlornly up the stairs, "Mary!"

There was no answer. She bounded up the stairs as if she was eighteen instead of fifty-five. For a long time there was utter silence at the top of the stairs. Then the governor heard them creak again as his wife descended heavily.

Her face was empty as she came into the parlor. He said, "She's dead, Emmy. I told you she was dead."

"How?" She looked at him numbly.

He had a compulsion to hurt her, as if Mary's death was her fault. He said, "She was shot. Out at that filthy abandoned Jaramillo shack."

"Shot? By who?"

"By Harvey TenEyck, that's who! What I want to know is why the hell I wasn't told she was going with that no good son-of-a-bitch! You must have known it. Probably everybody in town knew it, except me."

"Why would Harvey hurt her?"

"How should I know? I don't know how that no-good's mind works. All I know is that Mary's dead and King TenEyck's gun was layin' there beside her body when the sheriff found her a while ago."

The truth suddenly got through to Emmy Ludlow. It hit her like a sledge. She sank weakly into a platform rocker. Her skin was ghastly, a kind of greenish gray. Ludlow thought she was going to faint, but she didn't.

She stared emptily at nothing for a long, long time. Tears welled out of her eyes and ran silently across her cheeks. "Mary," she said. "I wonder where she is."

Ludlow said harshly, "Damn it, I told you she was dead."

She turned her head toward him as though with a supreme effort. She said almost soundlessly, "Harvey could have been your son. He could have been Mary's brother."

She was referring to King TenEyck's theft of his wife more than twenty years before. Harvey TenEyck's mother had still been his wife when Harvey had been born. He said, "Shut up! God damn it, shut your mouth."

"It's true." She had straightened in her chair. Color had returned to her face. Her eyes were suddenly bright with hate. "Harvey could have been *your* son if you'd been home where you belonged instead of up at the capital!"

He crossed to her in a couple of strides. His open hand swung, sharply striking the side of her face. The force of it snapped her head aside and left a red mark on her cheek.

She didn't move. She just stared up at him, her eyes unreadable but somehow malevolent.

He realized with a shock that Emmy hated him. Meek, submissive Emmy, who had always accepted whatever life had handed her, hated him. Her voice was scarcely audible. "What are you going to do?"

"I'm going to catch Harvey TenEyck, that's what

I'm going to do! I'm going to string the son-of-a-bitch up from the nearest tree!"

She nodded, as if she had expected his answer. He looked at her curiously. "What are *you* going to do?"

She said softly, "I'm going down to Phinney's and see her."

"And then?"

"I'm going to weep. I'm going to weep for those two lonely children who were both so afraid of their fathers they could never be anything but miserable."

"Then you knew!" he said triumphantly.

She nodded. "I knew."

"Why didn't you stop it, if you knew? Or why didn't you tell me?"

She didn't answer. She was no longer looking at him. It was as though he was not in the room, as though he did not exist.

He uttered a disgusted obscenity. He turned and went into the back parlor where the liquor cabinet was. He opened it and poured himself a tumbler half full of whiskey. He stared at it a moment then gulped it down. Damn King TenEyck! Damn Harvey! Damn! Damn!

He heard the stairs creak as Emmy went up to her room to dress. He heard water running and heard the toilet flush. After that he heard the stairs creak as she came down. He heard the front door open and close and he poured himself another drink.

He began to pace nervously back and forth. He was angry because of the way Mary had been killed, but he was already beginning to think of other things.

He was thinking that this might be the opportunity that had eluded him so long. This might be his chance to discredit King TenEyck so that TenEyck would never again be a threat to him.

Harvey had killed Mary, but TenEyck wasn't about to turn him over to the law. TenEyck would play God once more. Only this time his arrogance could be the seed of his destruction.

The U. S. Senate, denied Ludlow by TenEyck's influence, would be available. And beyond the U. S. Senate . . . He felt his heart begin to pound. The White House suddenly seemed within his reach.

He slammed down the whiskey glass, half its contents still unconsumed. He had better stop feeling sorry for himself and he had better stop dulling his wits with whiskey. He would need every bit of political acumen he possessed before this was over with. Several months remained before the elections in the fall. The party still had not nominated its candidate for the Senate. There was time to beat Arnold Ingraham.

The sympathy of the voters would be with a bereaved father at a time like this. Their sympathy would last long enough to assure his election in the fall. But TenEyck's influence had to be destroyed before he could be nominated.

He was roused from his thoughts by a pounding on the door. He hurried to open it.

Rork stood outside on the porch. Another patrolman, Simms, was with him. Ludlow said, "Come in. Come in." He held the door for Rork. Both men took off their hats and came inside.

Rork said, "Governor, King TenEyck's men have arrived in town. They're down at the hotel."

"How many?"

"Thirty. Forty. I didn't count."

Ludlow nodded. "All right. Let's go."

He left the light burning in the hall and followed the two state policemen out onto the porch. There was a predawn chill in the air. The eastern sky was lighter. He looked at his watch, but it was too dark to see its face.

Rork and Simms hurried down the street, with the governor between them. Ludlow discovered that he was shivering.

Rork said, "I'm sorry, Governor. How did Mrs. Ludlow take the news?"

The question snapped the governor out of his reverie. He said, "She was shocked, of course. She dressed and went down to the funeral parlor to see Mary's body." He supposed he should have accompanied his wife. Family solidarity, or at least the appearance of it was important at a time like this. "I'd have gone with her but . . ." He shuddered. "I guess I was overcome." He looked at Rork and then at Simms, to see how his explanation had gone over.

Both apparently accepted it at face value. Simms remained silent but Rork clucked sympathetically. "It's terrible, sir. It's just terrible."

"Do you think TenEyck has any idea where Harvey might have gone?"

"I doubt it, sir. If he knew where Harvey was, he wouldn't have needed all those men. I think he means to fan them out and search."

They reached Main Street at its upper end. Lights were burning in the lobby of the Elkhorn Hotel. In the glow they cast into the street, Ludlow could see the men milling around out front. They filled the street, their horses prancing nervously.

He continued to walk toward them, Rork and Simms staying close by his side. He could see now that some of the Crown hands were mounted, some standing on the ground.

King TenEyck stood on the hotel veranda facing them. He was talking to them but Ludlow was too far away to hear what he said. He stopped speaking, accepted the reins of a horse from someone and mounted heavily. He galloped down Main toward the depot and his men galloped after him. Their horses' hoofs filled the street with sound and dust. In minutes they were gone, their sound gone with them. The cloud of dust remained, a pall drifting slowly up the street.

Ludlow, Rork, and Simms reached the hotel. From out of the shadows the other state policemen came. Rork asked, "Where'd they go?"

No one seemed to know.

Rork asked, "What was he saying to them?"

"Just talk. He said Mary Ludlow had been killed and he thought the sheriff was going to blame his son. He said you were in town with some of your bully boys and he figured if you got your hands on Harvey you might take the law into your own hands. He wanted them to find Harvey before you did and he offered a hundred dollars to the man who found Harvey first."

"All right. Send two men after them. When they find out where TenEyck's going, one of them is to report back to me. The other is to keep right on following."

"Yes, sir." Rork called out two names. The men came forward and Rork passed on the governor's instructions to them. He said, "Get going. Don't lose them but don't get so close they know you're following. It will be light pretty soon and after that you shouldn't have any trouble."

The two men mounted and galloped away down the street in the direction TenEyck and his men had gone.

Rork asked, "Now what, Governor?"

"You come along with me. I want to talk to the sheriff and his deputy. There might be a chance one of them would know where TenEyck has gone."

With Rork at his side, he headed up the street toward the county courthouse, where the sheriff's office was.

The whole sky was a dingy gray. The breeze blew up the street, carrying with it a smell of the dust raised by King TenEyck's men and of the manure-littered livery stable corral beyond.

6.

Governor Ludlow led the way across the courthouse lawn and into the sheriff's office on the ground floor. The office was empty. He crossed it and opened the door leading to the cells.

There was a single light burning at the end of the stone corridor. A smell was in the place, of disinfectant and stale air. He could hear someone snoring and went toward the sound.

One of the cell doors stood open. Jesse Youngbear, the sheriff's deputy, was sleeping on the cot beneath the barred window of the cell. Governor Ludlow said harshly, "Deputy!"

Youngbear jerked awake, coming to a sitting position before he had completed opening his eyes. He reached for his gun and belt, lying on the floor beside the cot. Ludlow said, "I want to talk to you."

Youngbear looked up. His eyes were bloodshot and his hair tousled. He got to his feet, trying not to sound irritable. "Sure, Governor. Come on back to the office."

As he led the way down the corridor he said super-fluously, "I was up all night."

Ludlow didn't reply. Youngbear led the way into the office, then closed the door leading to the cells. He said, "Stinks in there but if a man gets tired enough he doesn't care."

Ludlow and Rork stood looking at him expression-less. Youngbear tried to be polite but irritation was growing rapidly in him. "What did you want to talk to me about?"

Ludlow said, "King TenEyck and his men just rode out of town. Have you got any idea where they might have gone?"

"Looking for Harvey, I suppose."

"Looking where?"

Youngbear asked, "How should I know, Governor?"

Rork said, "Watch it, Deputy."

Youngbear turned. He said thinly, "You watch it, Rork. What gives you the idea you can barge down here and start throwing your weight around? You woke me up. The goddam least you can do is be polite about it."

Ludlow said, "Deputy, I'm the governor of this state."

Youngbear said, "Then try to act like it." He was almost immediately sorry for that, so he said, "I know you're upset, Governor, and I don't mean to sound dis-respectful. But this knothead used to live down here and everybody knows him pretty well. They're not about to let him start pushing them around."

Rork's face was flushed. His eyes had narrowed and

he looked as if he'd like to kill Youngbear then and there. Ludlow said sharply, "Rork! Wait for me outside."

Rork glowered, then sullenly mumbled, "Yes, sir," and retreated to the door. He went out. He started to slam the door, thought better of it and closed it quietly. Ludlow said, "Now. Have you got any idea at all where King TenEyck might have gone?"

"Sure. I think I know where he went. Out to Daisy Kyle's."

"Why? Is Harvey there?"

"No, sir. But he was there earlier tonight. I had a hunch he might be and went out to get him. Daisy put a shotgun on me and Harvey got away."

"Which way did he go?"

Youngbear shrugged. "I don't know, Governor. It was dark, and like I said, Daisy had a gun on me."

"You must have been able to hear his horse's hoofs."

Youngbear said patiently, "Governor, right then I didn't give a damn which way he went. Daisy had a loaded shotgun in her hands and both hammers were cocked and she was shaking like a leaf. All I was thinking was that I'd better do everything she said or she'd blow a hole in me big enough to drive Si Ferguson's Maxwell through."

Ludlow made an understanding smile and nodded his head. He was now trying to placate the deputy, trying to smooth his ruffled feathers but it didn't quite come off. Youngbear suddenly understood why Ludlow had never been nominated to run for the Senate seat. He wasn't real. He was all front and no back. He had

fooled enough people to get himself elected to a series
of public offices and finally to the governorship, but
the party bigwigs weren't going to let him have the
Senate seat if they could possibly avoid doing so.

Youngbear also knew that Ludlow was going to use
this incident to further his political career if possible.
But how, he asked himself, could his daughter's death
further his political career?

Not by catching Harvey TenEyck and hanging him.
That would finish him politically. But if he let King
TenEyck find Harvey and take him back to Crown
. . . if TenEyck defied the law and refused to give
Harvey up for trial . . .

Ludlow said, "Thank you, Deputy." He was being
very pleasant now. He said, "I'm sorry about Rork. He's
a good man but sometimes he takes himself a bit too
seriously."

Youngbear nodded. He watched the governor go out
the door, his irritation stirring again. They'd waked him
up just to ask him a couple of stupid questions and
then they'd left. He wished he hadn't mentioned Daisy
Kyle. He shouldn't have. Ludlow could insist that she
be charged with aiding a fugitive.

He crossed to the door and opened it. The sun was
up. Too late to go back to sleep. He turned and stared
at the coffeepot. At least there was coffee and that
would help.

He poured himself a cup and sipped the scalding
stuff black. He found himself thinking of Daisy Kyle,
thinking of the way she had looked with that big double-

barrel in her hands, shaking like a leaf and scared half
to death. He grinned. He was damn fond of Daisy. He
supposed his mother would have a fit if he ever got
around to marrying her mostly because she had worked
in a saloon. But Youngbear knew she had worked as
a barmaid in the saloon and that was all. Daisy wasn't a
saloon girl. She didn't go upstairs with anybody and she
didn't meet anybody after hours outside the place.

Her father sometimes got pretty nasty with her about
the way she made her living but Youngbear didn't
figure he had any call to criticize. Daisy was a grown
woman. She wasn't doing anything wrong. And she *was*
supporting him.

He finished the coffee and went to the door. He
stepped out into the bright June sunlight. It was warm
and pleasant. Down in front of the Elkhorn Hotel he
could see the blue uniforms of Ludlow's state policemen. They untied their horses and mounted. The horses,
six of them, milled in the street briefly before their
riders lined them out toward the lower end of town
and dug spurs into their sides. The horses ran, thun-
dering across the Horse Creek bridge with a racket that
carried all the way to Youngbear, standing on the courthouse lawn.

One state policeman had stayed behind with the
governor. Now the two came walking up the street
toward the courthouse. Ludlow and the policeman,
Simms, crossed the lawn to where Youngbear stood.
Ludlow asked, "Can I use your phone?"

"Yes, sir. Help yourself." He followed the governor

into the sheriff's office. He supposed he ought to let Ludlow make his call in private, but he figured Chavez would expect him to know who Ludlow called and why. If Ludlow wanted privacy he could have made his call from the hotel.

Simms stayed outside, picking his teeth, soaking up the sun.

Ludlow cranked up the phone vigorously and spoke into it. "Get me the headquarters of the State Police in Denver."

He waited. He glanced at Youngbear and looked away again. Youngbear sat down in the sheriff's chair. It squeaked thunderously and Ludlow frowned.

After a moment he said, "Hello? This is Governor Ludlow, in Mesilla. I want you to send every available man down here on the next train. I also want you to contact Colonel Sanders of the State Militia and have him put his troops on alert. I may need a company or two on a few hours' notice. Have you got that?"

He listened a moment, nodded and said, "There is a train leaving Denver for Mesilla at ten. You should be able to round up thirty or forty men by then. Thank you." He replaced the phone on its hook.

Youngbear stood up. He said, "Joe Chavez isn't going to like your taking over the enforcement of the law. He's the sheriff and if you'll let him alone he'll find Harvey TenEyck and bring him in."

Ludlow frowned at him. "The way *you* did last night?"

Youngbear suppressed his irritation. Ludlow was entitled to the dig, he supposed. He *had* let Harvey get away. Maybe he could have gotten the gun away from Daisy without getting his head blown off. He just hadn't thought it important enough to take the chance. Harvey TenEyck wasn't going anywhere. There was no place he could go except out to Crown.

Besides, he was glad now that he hadn't brought Harvey back. TenEyck might have tried to force the jail and get him out. Ludlow and Rork might have done the same thing and if they had succeeded, might have lynched Harvey or gotten into a gunbattle with Ten-Eyck's men.

Ludlow stood there for several moments as though waiting for Youngbear to try justifying himself again. Youngbear didn't. He'd apologized once for letting Harvey get away. He wasn't going to keep on apologizing forever.

Ludlow went out, joined Simms and the two walked down the street toward the hotel. They were abreast of Phinney's Furniture Store and Funeral Parlor when a woman came out and joined them on the walk.

Even at this distance, even with a black scarf over her head, Youngbear recognized Governor Ludlow's wife. The two talked briefly and then Mrs. Ludlow went on, heading up the street toward home. She walked as if she was very tired, perhaps even faint.

Youngbear hurried out to the street, untied his horse and mounted him. He hurried after Mrs. Ludlow. The governor and Simms had disappeared into the hotel.

He caught up with Mrs. Ludlow while she was still two blocks from home. She was staggering and he dismounted and caught her arm. "Mrs. Ludlow? Are you all right?"

She glanced up at him. She smiled faintly. Her face was gray and covered with beads of sweat. She murmured, "Thank you, Jesse. I do feel a little faint."

He said, "I'll walk you home. Do you want me to get Doc Greenberg for you?"

"No. I'll be all right if I can just lie down a while." Her eyes blurred with tears. "It's a terrible shock, Jesse, seeing her like that."

"I know. I'm sorry, Mrs. Ludlow."

"Have you found Harvey yet?"

"No, ma'am. I found him last night but he got away from me."

She smiled faintly again. "I'm glad. I wouldn't want my husband to get hold of him." The smile faded. "I'm afraid it's more a matter of pride with him than grief."

"Yes, ma'am." They walked the rest of the distance in silence. She seemed steadier when Jesse left her at her door and she assured him she would be all right.

He mounted his horse and rode back toward town, frowning to himself.

7.

Sam Rork and five state patrolmen galloped out of town, heading toward Daisy Kyle's. Rork knew every inch of the country around Mesilla. He knew Crown ranch from one end to the other, almost as well as King TenEyck did. Sam Rork had been born and raised in Mesilla. He had worked for TenEyck on Crown from the time he was old enough to drive a stacker team at fifty cents a day.

But unlike most who had worked for Crown, Rork had bitterly resented the way wealth came so easily to King TenEyck. He had resented Harvey and the fact that someday all of it would belong to him, not because he had worked for it or because he was smart but just by an accident of birth, because Harvey was TenEyck's son.

Harvey TenEyck was even a bastard, born out of wedlock but that didn't matter. TenEyck acknowledged him and he would inherit Crown, while Sam, who worked hard, would never have more than day wages unless he got away from Mesilla and made something of himself on his own.

Well, he had made something of himself, he thought. He was chief of the State Police. He was a man of substance, a confidant of the governor. And if the governor became a senator . . . if he went on from there to eventually become president . . . then loyalty would pay off handsomely. Ludlow would take him to Washington. There would be a prestigious, well-paid job waiting for him there.

The trick, Rork had discovered, was to do each job well. No matter how big or how small it was.

Right now the governor wanted Harvey TenEyck. He wanted him in jail. He wanted Rork to find him before King TenEyck did. And that was what Sam Rork meant to do.

He arrived at the Kyle cabin a little after eight. Smoke curled from the tin chimney of the place. He spoke to his men. "A couple of you make a circle. Find out which way King TenEyck went."

A couple of the men rode off. Rork said, "Clegg, you and Donovan stay out here in the yard. If you see anybody coming, let me know. I don't want TenEyck surprising us."

The two men saluted and dismounted. They walked away from the house, leading their horses.

Rork swung to the ground and the remaining patrolman followed suit. They tied their horses to the corral fence and walked across the yard to the house. Rork knocked.

The door did not open. Instead, Daisy Kyle's voice called, "What do you want?"

Rork shouted, "State Police! Open up!"

There was no answer from Daisy Kyle. Rork repeated, "Open up! This is the State Police!"

Still there was no reponse from inside the house. Rork hesitated a moment, growing angry. He wanted to talk to Daisy. He knew he wasn't going to get anywhere following King TenEyck and his men. All he'd accomplish that way would be to verify that King TenEyck had found his son and taken him to Crown.

But if Daisy knew where Harvey had gone and if she could be made to tell . . . He might, perhaps, reach Harvey before TenEyck did. He could deliver him to the governor in town.

He turned to the man with him, a burly six-footer and said, "Break it open."

The other man looked at the door a moment. Then, stepping back, he delivered a kick just beside the knob. The door burst open with a resounding crash and Rork rushed through in time to yank a shotgun away from Daisy Kyle, standing white-faced in the middle of the room.

It discharged as he seized it, but the charge went harmlessly into the ceiling, blowing a ragged hole almost six inches across. Plaster sifted down from the hole. Rork broke the action of the gun and both spent shell and live one were ejected onto the floor. He spoke to the other man. "Go out and tell them everything's all right. Then come back."

Daisy's father sat helplessly in his chair. Daisy stood, white and shaking, in the middle of the room. The smell of sausage and flapjacks filled the air, which was warm and steamy from the stove and the water heating on the back of it.

Rork waited until the other patrolman, whose name was Clocker, returned. Then he asked, "Where'd he go, Daisy?"

Still shaking, she stared sullenly at him. "Where did who go?"

"Don't play games with me. Where did Harvey go?"

"I don't know where he went."

Rork felt a touch of irritation. He didn't like the steady way Daisy was looking at him. Almost with contempt. Certainly with unconcealed dislike.

He said, "The governor wants him. So does the law. He killed Mary Ludlow last night. He's a damn cowardly murderer. Now where did he go?"

She shook her head. "I don't know." Her eyes met his defiantly. "Even if I did know, I wouldn't tell the likes of you."

Rork didn't like being balked. He particularly didn't like being balked by a little saloon slut who had the gall to look at him like he was dirt, like he was one of King TenEyck's flunkies out at Crown. He swung a hand and the flat of it struck her on the side of the face with a resounding smack. Her father cursed suddenly and angrily, but Rork didn't even look at him. Daisy's head snapped to one side. She straightened. A red mark had appeared on her cheek.

Her eyes were blazing now. Her fear had disappeared. Rork shouted, "Damn you, where did Harvey go?"

Daisy looked him straight in the eye. She said evenly, "You can go straight to hell!"

Rork hit her again, this time so hard it knocked her to her knees. Furiously, he yanked her to her feet, with such violence that he tore the bodice of her dress. It exposed lacy underwear beneath and the upper third of each of her breasts.

Her father made a choking sound in his throat. He got to his feet with a superhuman effort and tried to take a step toward Rork. He sprawled headlong.

Daisy screamed, "Pa!" and tried to pull away and get to him. Rork hit her again, a slap with his right hand while he held her upper arm with his left.

Again her head snapped to one side. But she was fighting now. Her hands came up and her fingernails raked across Sam Rork's cheek from temple to jawline, bringing blood, leaving four long scratches that would not soon heal.

The pain was minor but the knowledge that she had marked him suddenly made Rork lose all control of himself. This time he hit her with his fist. It struck her just below the right eye and knocked her clear across the room. She banged against the stove and slid to the floor beside it, dazed.

Rork, raging, crossed the room and yanked her to her feet, once more tearing her dress and her underclothes beneath. Again he struck her, this time squarely in the mouth. Kyle was shouting curses, angered almost as much by his own helplessness as he was by Rork's brutality. Rork felt his arms seized from behind. Clocker shouted, "Sam! For God's sake, Sam! Stop it! Don't hit her any more!"

For several moments Rork struggled violently, trying to pull free. He cursed Clocker savagely, but Clocker held on. At last Rork made himself go limp. "All right, goddam it. All right! You can let go now."

Clocker released him. Daisy lay sprawled on the floor, dazed, unable to get up. Her father was trying to crawl to her, as if he could somehow protect her from further assault.

Rork was raging inwardly. He glared at Clocker and Clocker winced. He said defensively, "Sam, you could have killed her if I hadn't . . ."

"Shut up!" He knew there was no use remaining here. Not now. He had failed in his attempt to make Daisy talk. It was even possible that she didn't know where Harvey Ludlow was.

He stamped across the room and out into the morning sun. The two men he had stationed outside were down by the corral. They were looking curiously toward the house, no doubt having heard some of the commotion there. The other two were riding in from the north. They approached Rork and one of them, named Scappolini, said, "TenEyck's trail goes north. It sure don't look like Harvey was headed back to Crown."

"What about our two men?"

"One is still following. The other seems to have headed back toward town. We couldn't have missed him by very much. His trail cuts back about a mile from here."

Rork nodded. "All right, let's go. We'll follow Ten-Eyck until we make sure he's caught up with Harvey and taken him back to Crown. There's still an outside chance that we can get him first."

He walked to the corral and untied his horse. He mounted and rode out toward the north, following the plain trail of TenEyck and his men. The others fell in behind.

Rork was still angry at Clocker but he was glad now that Clocker had stopped him. He realized with a shock that he would have gone on beating Daisy Kyle until . . .

A cold sweat suddenly covered him. He might have killed Daisy if Clocker hadn't stopped him when he had.

His body, sweating, now turned cold. It was a terrible discovery to make about himself. God, he thought, I'm going to have to watch myself. Before my temper ruins everything.

Youngbear got his breakfast at the restaurant. By the time he had finished, he saw Joe Chavez turn into Main, ride to the hitchrail in front of the courthouse, dismount, and tie his horse.

He paid for his breakfast and went out into the street. He was frowning faintly, worrying about Daisy Kyle. He knew he shouldn't have told the governor about Daisy putting a gun on him last night so that Harvey could escape. Ludlow was angry enough to insist that Daisy be charged with aiding a fugitive.

But worry about Daisy being charged with a felony wasn't what was behind the nagging uneasiness he felt. He realized that he was worrying about her safety. He knew the methods of the State Police were sometimes brutal and direct. Ludlow was still in town but Rork and five state policemen had ridden out on the trail of King TenEyck and his men. That trail would take them straight to Daisy Kyle's.

Hurrying, he crossed the courthouse lawn on a path where the grass was worn away. He went into the sheriff's office. Chavez had a toothpick in his mouth. He was fresh shaven and had on a clean white shirt. He looked at his deputy, studying his face carefully. "Manage to get any sleep?"

"Not much. Ludlow woke me up."

"Where is he now?"

"I don't know. But he sent Rork and five others to follow TenEyck's trail."

Chavez grunted, "They won't start anything with Ten-Eyck's men. They're too badly outnumbered."

Youngbear agreed. But the nagging worry, the uneasiness remained in his mind. Chavez saw his frown and asked, "What's the matter?"

"I guess I'm worrying about Daisy Kyle and her old man. I told Ludlow about her putting a gun on me last night and letting Harvey get away. I'm afraid that Rork might try to make her tell him where Harvey went. I doubt if she knows but Rork might think she does."

"You don't think Rork would be stupid enough to hurt her, do you?"

Youngbear said, "You know Rork and so do I. He's got a hell of a temper. I saw him damn near kill a man once in a fist fight down at the Cowboy's Rest Saloon."

"Maybe you'd better go out and see."

Youngbear realized that this was what he had wanted Chavez to say. He felt a vast relief. He said, "I think I will."

He hurried out and untied his horse. The animal had been saddled all night but there wasn't time to change horses now. When he got back, he'd put the horse in the livery stable and get himself another one.

He rode out of town at a steady, rocking lope, a gait that swiftly ate the miles. The Kyle house looked peaceful enough when he brought it into sight. A wisp of smoke rose from the tin chimney. There was no activity in the yard. A hen cackled, announcing the fact that she had just laid an egg. A crow, high above, squawked raucously.

Youngbear rode in, dismounted, and dropped his horse's reins. He went to the door, which was partly open, and knocked.

Daisy answered it. One eye was swelling and already turning black. Her mouth was puffy and bleeding. She had been crying. Her cheeks were streaked with tears. But Youngbear could see that the crying was over with. Her eyes were blazing now.

His own chest felt tight. His fists had clenched themselves involuntarily. He wished Sam Rork was here right now because he wanted to give Rork what he'd given Daisy. He wanted that so bad it was a sour taste in his mouth.

Suddenly Daisy began to cry again. She ran to his arms and he closed them around her, holding her and letting her cry it out.

8.

It was a long time before Daisy stopped sobbing. Young-bear discovered he was a little sorry when she did. It had been pleasant holding her soft, warm body close to him. She stepped back, flushed a little, and put up a hand to brush tears from her eyes and smooth her hair. The eternal woman in her murmured embarrassedly, "I must look a mess."

Youngbear said, "You look fine to me. Except where that son-of-a-bitch hit you with his fists. I want you to sign a complaint. I'll throw him in jail."

Fear appeared suddenly in Daisy's eyes. The color drained out of her face. Numbly she shook her head.

Youngbear said, "There's nothing to be afraid of. He won't . . ."

Again Daisy shook her head. Her father said angrily, "Damn it, sign the complaint. Let Jesse put the bastard in jail."

Daisy continued to shake her head. Her father said,

"Then I'll sign it, Jesse. I can't come to town but you bring it out here next time you come."

Daisy turned pleading eyes on him, but he only scowled at her. She said, "Pa . . ." and stopped. He growled, "It's time some of the people around here found out we ain't dirt just because I'm crippled and you work in a saloon."

Youngbear said, "I'll get a complaint form and bring it out." He was embarrassed. For Daisy. He knew what her father thought about her working in the saloon. He muttered, "I've got to get back to town."

"I'll come outside with you," Daisy said.

He went out and she followed, pulling the door shut behind her. Her face was badly battered and he felt a wave of tenderness toward her. He put his arm around her shoulders as they walked toward his horse.

Reaching the horse, he released her and picked up the reins. His chest felt tight and his throat wanted to close, but he blurted the words out anyway, "I guess your pa would blow up if you told him you were going to marry a half-breed, wouldn't he?"

She looked up at him, her eyes startled. "You don't mean that. You're just sorry for me right now."

"Huh-uh. I've been thinking about it for quite a while." He hadn't, and he didn't know what had got into him. But it was too late to back away.

"What would your ma say if you married a saloon girl?"

"I don't reckon it's her business. It's mine."

"And I guess it's my business if I want to marry

a . . ." She couldn't say the term. He supplied it, grinning, "Half-breed."

She giggled. "My lips are split but you can kiss me if you're careful about it."

He leaned down and kissed her very lightly on the lips. She threw her arms around his neck and hugged him tight. She said, "Yes."

"Yes what?"

"I accept."

He felt a little scared. He hadn't intended to ask her to marry him today. But he had asked and she had accepted and now . . . But the prospect was decidedly pleasant, he discovered. Daisy asked, "When?"

"I don't know. After this business is settled. I guess. In the meantime, keep your door locked."

"I can't. Sam Rork kicked it open and broke the lock."

"I'll send someone out from town to fix it. Or maybe I'll fix it myself when I bring the complaint out this afternoon."

He leaned over and kissed her on the cheek. He mounted and grinned down at her. "See you later on this afternoon."

She nodded, her glance resting softly on his face. He realized that marrying her was going to put a lot of strain on what he earned as deputy. She couldn't go on working in the saloon and her father still had to be supported. But they'd manage. And he wouldn't be a deputy all his life.

He rode back to town at a steady trot, still surprised that he'd finally asked Daisy to marry him. He wondered what Joe Chavez would say. And he wondered what the sheriff's reaction would be when he told him he was going to throw Sam Rork in jail and charge him with assault.

Harvey TenEyck spurred frantically as he rode away from Daisy's house. He'd been startled when Daisy put a shotgun on Jesse Youngbear, thereby giving him this chance to get away. He shouldn't have been surprised, though. Daisy was notoriously softhearted. She was always feeding stray animals. She gave away a lot more of her salary than she could afford—to down-and-outers who needed a meal, or a bed, or even sometimes a drink to help get rid of the shakes.

She'd hold Youngbear long enough for him to get well away from the house and not even Youngbear could trail him in the dark.

He had no idea where he was going. Just so it wasn't back to Crown. He couldn't face his father. Never again.

He was sick with self-disgust. He'd been able to shoot Mary but when the time came to shoot himself, he'd found he was physically unable to pull the trigger.

He wished he was dead. But he wasn't. He was alive and that was maybe going to be harder than being dead.

Desperately he wished they'd never made that suicide pact. They'd been half out of their minds, wanting each other, wanting to be married and live together, and all the time knowing it wasn't possible. Too much bitterness, too much hatred was between their fathers, and

both men were too overwhelming, too powerful for them
to oppose successfully.

They had taken what had seemed, in a moment of
despair, to be the only way out. Now Harvey knew
they had been wrong. They could have run away. Or
they could have just faced their fathers and said they
were going to be married. Nothing could have been
worse than the way things were now. Mary was dead
and he was a murderer. Worse, he was a gutless,
spineless nothing that hadn't even had the courage to
carry out his part of the pact.

He found himself hoping that Youngbear *would* come
after him. He planned what he would do. He'd force
Youngbear to kill him. He'd make Youngbear think he
was going to shoot him and he'd force the deputy to
kill him in self-defense.

Steadily north he rode. That plan wouldn't work,
he realized, because Youngbear wasn't afraid of him.
Youngbear would never believe that he would really
shoot.

He traveled for about ten miles before he pulled his
heaving horse to a halt. He had just climbed the side
of a bluff. The moon was up and he could see for miles.
He could even see pinpoints of light out there in the
distance southward and knew they must be the arc
lights on Main Street in Mesilla.

He dismounted, dropped the reins, then loosened
the cinch so the horse could breathe more easily. He
withdrew the rifle from the saddle scabbard and looked
at it. On impulse, he levered a shell into the chamber.

He put the butt on the ground in front of him. Bending forward, he put the muzzle in his mouth. He put his thumb through the trigger guard.

He began to sweat. His body felt as if it was drenched, and he felt awfully cold. He began to tremble violently. He tried to force his thumb hard against the trigger. He failed. He tried again and failed again.

He flung the rifle away from him. Sobs shook him and he sank to his knees. He wished he was dead. He wanted to be dead. But he couldn't kill himself.

Forgetting the rifle, he groped for his horse's reins, found them, mounted and drummed heels against the horse's sides. Perhaps frightened by his strange behavior, the horse thundered away. Harvey kept drumming against his sides with his heels. He belabored the horse's rump with the ends of the reins, as if only speed could carry him away from himself away from his shame and guilt.

Across the top of the bluff the terrified animal ran. He reached the other side, where rimrock was five or six feet high.

The horse tried to stop and could not. He planted his feet and slid. As he went over the edge, he uttered a shrill sound of terror.

The horse plummeted down, striking the steep slope below the rim still on his feet, but losing his footing immediately and rolling toward the bottom. Harvey was flung clear, and he too rolled helplessly down the slope, but behind the horse because his weight was less.

His head struck a rock and for an instant the world

whirled. He had time to think that he'd gotten his wish. He was dying. And then everything went black.

The sun was well up in the sky when King TenEyck led his men up the steep slope of the bluff toward the narrow line of rimrock at the top. He climbed out at the same place Harvey had, and spotted the rifle almost immediately.

He dismounted and picked it up. The hammer was cocked and there was a live shell in the chamber. Ten-Eyck unloaded it and tossed it to Dan Malloy. "Where'd he get that?"

"Daisy's place, probably."

TenEyck understood why the gun had been loaded. He understood the marks he had seen on the ground nearby. Harvey's bootprints. The deeply indented mark of the gun butt just in front of where the bootprints were. Harvey had once more tried to kill himself. Once more he had failed.

TenEyck followed Harvey's tracks to the place where he had mounted his horse. He noted the way the horse had literally sprung away, running almost immediately. He frowned as he mounted his own horse and followed, sensing if not wholly understanding Harvey's anguish at his failure to kill himself. In King TenEyck's world when a man really wanted to do something he did it. In his mind if Harvey really wanted to kill himself he would have done it last night at the Jaramillo place.

He reached the other rim and saw instantly where Harvey's horse had gone off the rim. He looked down the slope, picking out the body of the horse first, that of Harvey almost immediately afterward.

He found a break in the rim where his horse could slide down and forced him to take it. He dismounted beside Harvey, glanced up at Malloy and said, "That horse is still kicking. Take care of it."

Malloy slid down to where Harvey's mount lay, alive and in pain, kicking occasionally. He raised the rifle TenEyck had tossed him back on top of the bluff and put a bullet into the horse's head. Then he turned and climbed his horse back to where TenEyck and the others were.

TenEyck was kneeling beside Harvey. The boy was dusty, scratched, and bloody but he wasn't dead. There was a knot on the side of his head as big as a walnut from which blood had oozed and dried. He groaned and stirred as TenEyck rolled him onto his back. After a few moments he opened his eyes.

They were strange and wild-looking at first. TenEyck's face was harsh, the way it had always been when he looked at his son. He was strong and hard. He took what he wanted and if rules or laws interfered he broke them without thinking twice. He could understand almost anything but weakness. Harvey was weak, and he had never understood Harvey any more than Harvey had understood him.

But there was something else in TenEyck's mind and heart even if it didn't show in his eyes. It was a tortured longing to understand. Harvey was his son, for all his weakness, for all his shortcomings. And he loved his son, as much as he was capable of loving anything.

Harvey's eyes focused on his face. They met Ten-Eyck's briefly, and as always looked away. TenEyck said, "Why? For God's sake, why?"

Harvey's face flushed slightly. He rolled, and struggled to sit up. He got to his hands and knees on the rocky slope, head hanging in obvious pain. TenEyck repeated, "Why?"

Harvey looked up at him. He met his father's glance and this time he did not look away. TenEyck had never seen such hatred in anyone nor had he seen such fury. Harvey choked, "Why? I'll tell you why. Because you and the governor hate each other so God damn much you'd have killed us yourselves before you'd have let us be together."

TenEyck knew that was true. At least it was true of the governor, if it was not of him. Ludlow's hatred was murderous and unforgiving and it hadn't diminished with the years. He'd have sent Mary off to Europe or New York if he'd so much as suspected she had been seeing Harvey. He'd have kept her there. And if that didn't work, he'd have had his State Police take care of Harvey, one way or another, not excluding having him beaten half to death or killed if nothing else would work. No. Harvey was right. He and Mary could never have had a life together.

He asked harshly, "Then why didn't you kill yourself after you killed her?"

The fury went out of Harvey's eyes as quickly as it

had appeared in them, to be replaced by shame. Ten-Eyck repeated, "Why?"

"I couldn't." The words were scarcely audible. "I couldn't. I tried to pull the trigger but I couldn't." Harvey suddenly began to sob. His shoulders shook. His head dropped and his face buried itself in the dirt and crumbled rock on the slope. He didn't seem to know or care.

TenEyck stood looking down at him. Disgust mingled with pity in his face. Love warred with contempt in his confused mind. He was thinking that he ought to abandon Harvey to his fate. He ought to turn him over to the law.

Yet he knew that he would not. In the first place, the law couldn't hold him, couldn't give him a fair trial. Governor Ludlow, backed by the power of his State Police, was too strong.

And in the second place, he couldn't let Ludlow win. He couldn't let Ludlow beat him now, after all these years.

He turned to Dan Malloy. "Put him up behind one of the men, and bring him home."

He mounted and rode back to the top of the bluff. Alone, he rode toward Crown. He was thinking about Harvey's mother and of the way that she had died. There had been no physical explanation for her death. She had simply died of shame.

He had never been a religious man. But now he wondered if he was not being punished for so ruthlessly taking Ludlow's wife twenty years ago.

He shook himself impatiently. He was acting like an old woman, and he had better snap out of it. Ludlow would bring to bear every bit of power available to him, including the State Militia. Keeping Harvey from falling into his hands might well be the hardest thing that TenEyck had ever done.

9.

It was past midmorning when Youngbear reached town. He rode directly to the courthouse. No Crown men were visible nor were any members of the State Police. Mesilla drowsed in the summer sun. A buggy moved sedately down Main. Si Ferguson's Maxwell was parked in front of the Elkhorn Hotel, its engine idling. A dog stood on the courthouse lawn, looked at Youngbear and idly wagged its tail at him.

He crossed the lawn and went into the sheriff's office. Chavez was sitting in his swivel chair, feet up on the desk. He was smoking a twisted black Mexican cigar. Layers of cigar smoke hung motionless in the air.

Youngbear straddled a straight-backed chair, rested his arms on its back and stared at the sheriff. "That son-of-a-bitch Rork worked Daisy over with his fists. She's scared to sign a complaint but her old man isn't. I want to type one up and take it out there this afternoon."

Chavez stared thoughtfully at the tip of his cigar. Youngbear said, "Well?"

Chavez shrugged. "It's Kyle's privilege, I guess, to make a complaint."

"What do you mean, it's his privilege? Rork beat Daisy up with his fists. You ought to see her face."

Chavez studied him. "I know how you feel. You're kind of stuck on Daisy, aren't you?"

Youngbear said, "I just finished asking her to marry me."

"And?"

Youngbear grinned. "She said she would."

"Congratulations."

Youngbear frowned faintly. "What's the matter with you, Joe?"

Chavez hesitated a moment. Then he said forcefully, "Filing a complaint against Rork would be a damn big mistake."

"Why? There's two witnesses against him."

"And five or six State Police that will call Daisy and her pa a pair of liars. You know a jury will believe a policeman more times than not."

"But Daisy . . ."

Chavez said, "You won't like what I'm going to say but it's got to be said. Daisy works in a saloon. She ain't married. The lawyers the governor hires to defend Rork will put her on trial instead of Rork."

"What do you mean by that?" There was an edge to Youngbear's voice.

"I mean they'll tear her to shreds. They'll ruin her reputation. They'll make people believe she's somethin' both you and I know she ain't. Rork will get off scot-free, and Daisy will be ruined. Is that what you want?"

Scowling, Youngbear shook his head. He was furious at the injustice of it but he knew what the sheriff said was true. He growled angrily, "Then Rork can go around beating women up and there's nothing we can do?"

Chavez didn't answer him. There was no need. Youngbear was just giving voice to his resentment and both of them knew his words for what they were.

A distant train whistle made Youngbear cock his head. He looked at the office clock. The train was early. It wasn't due until close to one.

Both knew the train was early because it was loaded with members of Governor Ludlow's State Police. Chavez breathed, "Oh Lordy. Here it comes," and Youngbear knew he wasn't talking about the train but about the trouble its passengers would bring with them.

Chavez got to his feet. The chair squeaked thunderously. He said, "Let's walk down and meet the train. I wouldn't mind knowing what we're up against."

Youngbear followed him out the door. He was still disgruntled about Rork getting off scot-free, but he had to admit Chavez was right. Maybe he'd get a chance to settle the score with Rork himself. If he ever caught Rork without half a dozen of his State Police to back him up.

They walked down Main toward the depot at its lower end. Si Ferguson, wearing a checked cap and goggles, drove his Maxwell down the street ahead of them, dust raising from its yellow wheels. He stopped in front of the depot and sat there watching the train approach.

Heat was building up in the street. Clouds were already beginning to form over the high peaks in the distance west of town, promising a thunderstorm later on this afternoon.

The engine puffed into the station and stopped with a great screeching of brakes and the hiss of escaping steam. The blue-uniformed conductor put the step out and the passengers began to alight. An elderly woman came first, followed by the usual collection of midday passengers. There were about fifteen in all. When the last of them had alighted, the State Police began to disembark.

Youngbear counted absently as they came down the steps. By the time he had finished, Governor Ludlow and Simms had arrived from the hotel. Chavez asked, "How many did you count?" and Youngbear said, "Forty-three."

Chavez walked to the governor. He said, "Governor Ludlow, Sam Rork beat up Daisy Kyle this morning, trying to make her tell where Harvey TenEyck had gone."

The governor looked coldly at him. "Don't tell me about it. Arrest Rork. Charge him with assault.'"

Chavez shook his head. The governor asked, "Why not?"

"Because I know what you and Rork would do to Daisy Kyle." He waited a moment, meeting the governor's glance steadily. At last he said, "Governor, don't let this get out of hand. Go back to Denver and take these men with you. I'll get Harvey TenEyck. I'll see that he stands trial."

"Like your deputy got him last night, I suppose." Ludlow's voice was contemptuous.

Chavez flushed slightly. Youngbear started to open his mouth, then closed it. Chavez said, "I don't think you want Harvey brought to trial. You don't want your daughter's killer brought to justice. You want to use this whole miserable thing to further your career. You think that if you can discredit King TenEyck, or have him killed, you can get the nomination for U. S. Senator."

Governor Ludlow flushed. For a moment he glared at the sheriff and his deputy. Then he turned and stalked up Main Street, the State Police following. The whole group crowded into the hotel.

Chavez didn't move until the last of them had disappeared. Then he said, "Come on. I think we'd better find out if King TenEyck's found Harvey yet."

"And what if he has? Once he gets Harvey out to Crown, he'll never give him up."

"Maybe not, but it won't hurt to ask. He might be so ashamed of Harvey he'll let him take his own chances with the law."

Youngbear grinned. "That doesn't sound much like King TenEyck to me."

Chavez grinned back. "No, it doesn't, does it? Come on."

The pair walked up the street, both intensely aware

of their helplessness. If Ludlow decided to take the law into his own hands, there would be little the sheriff and his deputy could do.

Inside the sheriff's office, Chavez went to the phone. He cranked vigorously and a moment later said, "Myrtle, ring Crown for me. I want to talk to King TenEyck if he's there."

He thought her voice sounded a little scared, but he could hear the phone tinkling out at Crown. After several moments a harsh voice said, "Hello!"

Chavez said, "Mr. TenEyck?"

"Yeah."

"This is Joe Chavez. Did you find Harvey? Have you got him there at Crown?"

"What if I have?"

"Then you *have* got him there?"

"All right. I have. What about it?"

"I want him for murder, Mr. TenEyck. I want you to surrender him."

"Yeah. I guess you do. Well you can go to hell. You know what will happen if I surrender him. That bunch of blue-uniformed flunkies of Ludlow's will string him up to the nearest tree."

"I won't permit that, Mr. TenEyck."

TenEyck snorted contemptuously. "You couldn't stop it and you damn well know it."

"Then you won't surrender him?"

"Hell no, I won't. Not until there's at least some guarantee that he'll he tried, not lynched."

"You know what Governor Ludlow will do, don't you?"

"I don't care what he does."

✦ Chavez's patience was wearing thin but he knew it would do no good to lose his temper with King TenEyck. He said, "He'll try to take him by force, that's what he'll do. And I can't stop him. There's only me and Jesse Youngbear and Ludlow has got fifty men of the State Police."

"Let the son-of-a-bitch try to take Harvey away from me by force. Just let him try that. I've got a hundred and fifty men."

"You want a war, Mr. Ten Eyck?"

"No, I don't want a war. And I won't start one. But I'll fight if I'm attacked."

Chavez could see he wasn't getting any place. He shook his head wearily at Jesse Youngbear as he said, "All right, Mr. TenEyck," and hung up the phone.

The door opened and a tall, elderly man came in. He was thin and distinguished looking, wearing a dark suit and gray felt hat. His hair was white and he wore it a bit long in back. Joe Chavez said deferentially, "Hello, Senator." He crossed the room and extended his hand. "What brings you down here?"

Jesse Youngbear had seen pictures of Arnold Ingraham in the newspapers but he'd never seen him face to face. Ingraham glanced at him and Chavez said, "This is Jesse Youngbear, my deputy."

Ingraham crossed the office and shook hands with

Youngbear. He was a courtly old man, dignified and self-possessed. He had a genuine warmth and, Youngbear thought, that was probably why he had served so many terms, always being re-elected with a large plurality. Ingraham said, "Have you arrested Harvey TenEyck yet?"

Chavez shook his head. "King TenEyck has him out at Crown and refuses to surrender him."

"What are you going to do?"

"Nothin' I can do, I guess. Right now at least. I'd waste my time trying to take him away from all the men TenEyck's got out at Crown."

"And the governor?"

"He's ridin' high, Senator. He's in the right and he knows it. He's going to make all the political hay he can out of this. He's going to get rid of TenEyck one way or another. He'll get him charged with harboring a fugitive or he'll get him killed. Either way, TenEyck will lose just about all the political influence he has."

Ingraham nodded. He said, "I think I'll hire a rig and drive out to Crown. Maybe there is something I can do to help."

Chavez said, "Jesse, go down to the stable and get the senator a rig. Get him a driver too."

Youngbear headed for the door.

10.

Rork and his men got back to town at one. They rode up the street and drew rein in front of the Elkhorn Hotel. They tied their horses and tramped inside.

Jesse Youngbear saw them arrive. Chavez had gone to dinner and was due back at any time.

Youngbear thought of the bruises on Daisy's face and the more he thought about it the madder he got. Rork had beaten Daisy and legally there was nothing either he or the sheriff could do about it. The governor and Rork would ruin Daisy's reputation if Rork was brought to trial. Rork was going to get away with it. Unless . . .

Youngbear left the office. He knew Chavez wouldn't approve of what he was going to do. He knew it was foolish. But he also knew he was going to do it no matter what the consequences were.

He walked quickly down Main to the hotel. It was like a State Police convention. The lobby was full of blue uniforms. Governor Ludlow was sitting on a leather-covered sofa, with Rork sitting at his side.

Youngbear was aware that he could easily get himself killed right here in the lobby of the Elkhorn. But he was betting that the governor wouldn't permit a killing. So far he was in the right. If he let his State Police kill a local law officer, his aura of righteousness would be gone.

Youngbear went straight to the sofa where Rork and the governor sat. Ludlow looked up at him. He nodded. "Hello, Governor."

He realized his hands were shaking. He wanted to kill Rork—with his bare hands. He said, "Do you want it here, Rork, or do you want to go outside?" He hadn't missed the marks Daisy's nails had left on Sam Rork's face.

Ludlow said sharply, "Deputy! There'll be no fighting here. Rork was wrong in doing what he did. But after all, she's only a saloon girl."

Rork had gotten to his feet. Ludlow's words released something in Youngbear's mind. He hit Rork in the mouth and had the satisfaction of feeling teeth give before his fists. Rork slammed backward into the sofa and catapulted over its back. Youngbear didn't wait for him to get up. He dived over the sofa after him, landing on his hands and knees.

Rork was trying to get up but he was momentarily stunned by the blow. Youngbear beat him to his feet and slammed a fist into his mouth a second time. Rork went back again, skidding on the white tile floor. He rolled and, facing away from Youngbear, came to his hands and knees, noisily spitting teeth.

Youngbear booted him in the rump with enough force to drive him forward, sprawling. Rork's face skidded along the floor. His head banged against a polished brass spittoon, which overturned, drenching him with its contents.

Still stunned, he staggered to his feet, the stains of the overturned spittoon on his face and on the front of his uniform. He wiped his face with a sleeve, his eyes glared at Youngbear murderously. And now, suddenly, he went for the gun hanging at his side.

The holster was high, a flap snapped over the gun. The flap delayed him long enough for Youngbear to swing a long blow at Rork's mid-section. Despite the man's condition, his fist sank two inches into Rork's unprotected belly and drove an explosive grunt from him. Youngbear had no intention of letting this turn into a gunfight. As Rork doubled, he brought up a knee. With near perfect timing, it caught Rork squarely in the face.

Rork's nose was smashed. What teeth remained in front were either broken or driven back. Nearly unconscious, he collapsed to the floor, blood streaming from his nose and mouth.

Ludlow was screeching excitedly. Youngbear felt his arms seized by half a dozen men. Rork lay on the blood-stained white-tile floor, in the pool left by the overturned spittoon. Youngbear glared down at him with satisfaction. No matter what happened now, he had this much. He had returned what Rork had done to Daisy Kyle twofold. And Rork hadn't laid a fist on him.

He was out of breath but he couldn't help the grin that spread across his face. He looked at the governor challengingly.

Ludlow said, "Let him go."

The policemen holding Youngbear stared at the governor unbelievingly. Ludlow repeated, "Let him go!"

Youngbear felt his arms released. Panting slightly, he said, "You may be the governor, but you're not the law in this county. Next time one of your bully boys breaks the law, it'll go harder on him than this."

He glanced once more at Rork, lying stunned on the lobby floor. He turned and walked a little unsteadily through the sea of blue uniforms to the door.

His knuckles were bleeding and he raised them to his mouth absently. He stepped out into the sunlight, grinning with the satisfaction that he felt. Chavez might not approve of what he had done but he had a hunch Chavez wouldn't protest too much.

He wondered what was going to happen now. Ten-Eyck had Harvey safely out at Crown, but Governor Ludlow was a long ways from giving up.

Still grinning, Youngbear walked up the street. Chavez met him in front of the courthouse. "What are you grinning about?"

He noticed Youngbear's knuckles then and asked, "Rork?"

Youngbear nodded.

"You're damn lucky you didn't get yourself killed. Did you start the fight?"

Youngbear nodded, trying not to look too smug.
"With the lobby full of state cops?" Chavez's voice
was incredulous.

Youngbear nodded again.

"I ought to fire you. I never heard anything so damn
stupid in my life." Chavez looked at him disgustedly.
"But it don't look like he laid a glove on you."

Youngbear said, "He didn't."

Chavez shrugged. "All right. But don't pull anything
like that again."

Youngbear shook his head. Silently he followed
Chavez across the courthouse lawn to the door of the
sheriff's office. The two of them went inside.

Rork got to his knees, shaking his head to clear it.
He looked up at the governor, trying to wipe the blood
and the spittoon's contents off his face and the front
of his shirt. Ludlow said coldly, "Go get yourself cleaned
up."

Rork muttered thickly, "I'll kill the son-of-a-bitch!"

"Shut up. You'll kill nobody. And from now on
you'll do what I tell you to and only what I tell you to.
You'll beat up no more women. You'll take nothing on
yourself."

"I thought you wanted Harvey TenEyck. I figured
that damn slut could tell me where he'd gone."

Ludlow said, "Get yourself cleaned up. Then come
back."

He watched Rork shuffle across the lobby to the stairs.
A Mexican woman brought a pail of water and a mop

and began to clean up the lobby floor. She glanced up once at Ludlow, apparently awed, then went silently back to her work.

Rork was gone twenty minutes. When he returned, he had on a clean shirt. He was dabbing at his lacerated face with a handkerchief. Every time he opened his mouth he winced with the pain as air hit the broken stubs of his teeth. "I've got to get to a dentist. These damn teeth are killing me."

"Later. Sit down. It's time we talked."

"About what?"

"About what we're going to do."

"It's simple enough. We go out there to TenEyck's place and take Harvey away from him."

Ludlow shook his head. "Huh-uh. We demand that the sheriff capture him and bring him in to jail. The sheriff can't or won't, but we give him a chance to try."

"And then?" Rork was scowling.

"We let the newspapers know that TenEyck refuses to give his son up, in open defiance of the law. We get a warrant charging him with harboring a fugitive. We get the sheriff to serve the warrant. When TenEyck tears it up, which he will, we let the newspapers know that too."

Rork's eyes were interested now. Ludlow said, "Then we call out the State Militia. I can declare that a state of insurrection exists. We march out to Crown headquarters and give TenEyck a chance to surrender himself and his son."

"He won't."

"Of course he won't. And we don't want him to. We

let him fire a few shots at the Militia and then we withdraw. We let the newspapers know we want no civil war in Colorado. By then we ought to have full public sympathy."

"But you can't let him get away with it. That sure as hell won't get you any votes."

"He's not going to get away with anything. Next I appeal to Senator Ingraham to use his influence with TenEyck. I do it publicly and give the text of my appeal to the newspapers."

Rork grinned. "And that tars the senator with the same brush."

"Right. And since all appeals to reason have now failed, I announce that I have no choice but to uphold the sovereign authority of the governor. I lead the Militia and the State Police against Crown."

"We'll play hell taking Crown headquarters. With a hundred and fifty men defending it. It's like a damn fortress. It could hold out for months."

"We won't attack Crown headquarters. We'll attack one or both of the towns where the ranchhands' families live. That will pull the defenders away from Crown. Once we've done that, we can attack Crown headquarters."

"You going to hang Harvey TenEyck when you capture him?"

Ludlow shook his head. "King TenEyck is going to get killed in the fight. We'll take Harvey prisoner. We'll see that he's jailed and brought to trial. He'll hang. With his father dead, he'll hang. There's no doubt of it."

Rork grinned again, then winced when the air hit his teeth. He mumbled again, "I got to find a dentist."

Ludlow nodded. "Go ahead. I just wanted you to know the plan. I don't want any more stupidity like beating women up."

Rork nodded. He got up and crossed the lobby to the door. He went out into the street.

Scarcely had he disappeared when Chavez came in, alone. He crossed the lobby to the governor. "I'm going to ask you once more, Governor. Send these men back to the capital. I'll take care of arresting Harvey TenEyck and bringing him to jail."

Ludlow shook his head. "I have no intention of going back or of sending back any of my men. But I do demand you go out to Crown immediately and put Harvey TenEyck under arrest."

Chavez said, "I won't bring him to town as long as you men are here. I'm not a fool. I know what you'd do to him."

"Then I have no choice but to give the entire story to the newspapers. And futhermore, I intend to swear out a warrant charging King TenEyck with harboring a fugitive. I suppose you'll refuse to serve that too?"

Chavez scowled at him. Chavez wasn't a fool and he knew the governor had a carefully thought out plan. But he didn't say anything because he could see it wasn't going to do any good. With an angry shrug, he turned and tramped across the lobby to the door.

11.

It was late afternoon when Chavez returned to the sheriff's office. He found Youngbear nervously pacing back and forth. The deputy glanced questioningly at him, and Chavez shook his head. "He's just as bull-headed as TenEyck is. He won't send them back. He's got a plan."

"What kind of plan?"

"He's going to bring the newspapers into it, and use the thing to make some political hay. I don't think he wants his daughter's killer near as bad as he wants Senator Ingraham's Senate seat."

"Then maybe Harvey *would* be safe in jail. If we could get King TenEyck to give him up."

Chavez shrugged. "Might be. But TenEyck never would."

"Why don't I ride out there and see?"

Chavez hesitated. He knew it would be a gamble—bringing Harvey to the Mesilla jail. He doubted if Ludlow would risk his political future by letting his

State Police lynch the boy, but he couldn't be absolutely sure. He said, "Go on out to Crown. I'll call Denver and see what I can do about getting a U.S. marshal and deputy to come down here."

Youngbear went out. He had exchanged his horse for a fresh one at the livery stable when he hired a rig for Senator Ingraham earlier. Now he untied the fresh horse, a dappled gray, and swung astride. He headed south out of town, taking the road that led past the Jaramillo shack toward Crown.

Passing the shack where the murder had occurred, he stared at it briefly, noting absently that the door was closed. He remembered Mary Ludlow, a pretty if overly solemn girl, and he remembered Harvey TenEyck. It suddenly occurred to him that he couldn't recall ever having heard either of them laugh.

Shaking off the thought, he touched the gray's sides with his heels. The animal began to singlefoot, to Youngbear's pleased surprise. It was an easy gait on a man, and one that covered the distance almost as rapidly as a trot.

He thought of Daisy and a little smile touched his mouth. He liked to think about Daisy, but thinking of marriage made him nervous and put an empty feeling into his stomach.

There was a gate across the left fork of the road about five miles south of town. Over the gate hung a sign bearing the words CROWN RANCH. Below, the Crown brand had been burned into the wood with a running iron.

He opened the gate without dismounting, rode

through and closed it behind him. The sun was dipping toward the snow-covered peaks in the west but there were still several hours of daylight left.

He traveled another couple of miles before he saw the first of the towns where the families of Crown's married crewmen lived. It lay to his right against a long finger of ridge that slanted toward the road. It was about a mile away but he could see smoke rising from some of the chimneys and he could see people moving about. There was no way TenEyck could defend it, he thought. Not and defend Crown headquarters and the other, smaller town beyond. Not if Ludlow decided upon an all-out attack.

But could he risk an all-out attack, Youngbear asked himself. The answer was no. Not now at least. Not until all other possibilities had been exhausted.

Frowning, he tried to make himself think the way Ludlow must be thinking. Chavez had said that Ludlow didn't want Harvey brought to justice nearly as much as he wanted to use the killing of his daughter to obtain Ingraham's Senate seat for himself. And how could he best accomplish that?

The answer was obvious. He neither wanted Harvey TenEyck arrested and brought to trial nor did he want him lynched. He wanted King TenEyck to do just what he was doing. He wanted TenEyck to defy the law. He wanted TenEyck's defiance of the law publicized from one end of the state to the other. Then and only then could he move on Crown with impunity.

But if the sheriff and his deputy were able to per-

suade TenEyck to surrender his son for trial . . . That
would take all the wind out of Ludlow's sails. That
alone could spoil his plan.

It was six o'clock when Youngbear rode into the yard
at Crown. A dozen men could be seen moving about the
yard.

Crown headquarters consisted of perhaps twenty or
twenty-five buildings in all. Dominating them was the
house, a huge, three-story building of native stone.
Originally it had been a big square block of a house
but in recent years log and frame additions had been
tacked onto three sides and a wide veranda on the
fourth, giving it a kind of rustic charm.

Behind it, a log barn towered. Scattered on both
sides and behind the barn were other buildings, store-
houses, the bunkhouse, the icehouse, chicken houses,
garages, and machinery sheds. King TenEyck didn't
own an automobile, but he did own several trucks, and
there were at least half a dozen big steam tractors either
here or scattered across the miles of bottomland on
Crown.

West of the house flowed the Sangre de Cristo River,
wide and clear and lined with trees. Beyond the river
were hay meadows dotted with brown stacks of hay.

Nobody paid any attention to Youngbear. He rode
straight to the house, dismounted, and tied his horse.

There had once been a small plot of grass in front
of the house, but it had died for lack of care. A low
picket fence still enclosed the plot. Youngbear went

up the gravel walk to the door. He gave the bell a vigorous twist and heard it ring inside the house.

He waited for what seemed a long time before the door opened. King TenEyck stood in the doorway, scowling.

Youngbear said, "I want to talk to you."

"Talk away."

Youngbear frowned. It wasn't easy talking to a man like this but it didn't look like he was going to be invited in. He said, "The sheriff wants you to surrender your son. He's going to try and get a U.S. marshal and deputy down here from Denver to help us guard the jail."

TenEyck continued to scowl at him. "I told Chavez I wasn't going to surrender him. Not until he could give me some kind of guarantee that Ludlow's thugs wouldn't string him up."

"A U.S. marshal and deputy should be guarantee enough. Ludlow wouldn't dare . . ."

TenEyck laughed harshly. "He'd dare anything if he thought he could get to me."

Youngbear glimpsed another man behind TenEyck. The man came to the door. It was Senator Ingraham. Youngbear said stubbornly, "The governor doesn't want Harvey nearly so bad as he wants you, Mr. TenEyck. You're what's standing in his way and if he can he'll use this trouble to get at you. Giving Harvey up would make that impossible."

Ingraham said, "He's right."

TenEyck scowled. "The hell with that. They'd take

him out and string him up before he'd been in jail an hour."

Youngbear knew there was no use trying to persuade TenEyck to change his mind. He also knew better than to suggest that TenEyck send along enough of his men to guarantee Harvey's safety as long as he was in jail. That would only invite a civil war.

He said, "The governor intends to swear out a warrant charging you with harboring a fugitive. The sheriff will have no choice but to serve it as soon as it's given to him."

"Let him try," Ten Eyck growled.

Youngbear felt a touch of exasperation. He said, "Can't you see that you're playing right into Ludlow's hands? He *wants* you to defy the warrant. He *wants* you to refuse to surrender Harvey to the law. It will give him the excuse he needs to attack you."

"I got a hundred and fifty men."

"Sure you have. And you've got two towns and a ranch headquarters to defend, haven't you? And maybe two or three hundred haystacks. And sawmills. And cattle. There are a hundred ways he can hurt you and make you spread out your hundred and fifty men. Then he can cut you up."

"With those thugs he calls his State Police?" TenEyck's voice was an angry growl, but for the first time there was doubt in it.

Youngbear shook his head. "With the State Militia. He's the governor. He can declare a state of insurrection. That will give him an excuse to use the Militia."

TenEyck hesitated only an instant. Then he seemed to stiffen. "Go tell Chavez my answer is still no. I'll be damned if I give Harvey to those wolves. And tell Chavez if Ludlow comes out here, he'd better be prepared to lose some men. I'm goin' to give orders to shoot to kill."

Youngbear could see it was no use arguing. Shrugging, he turned away. He went down the walk and untied his horse. He mounted and rode toward town, holding the horse to a steady lope.

Tomorrow, Ludlow would get the judge to issue a warrant for TenEyck's arrest. He might even get it done tonight, by virtue of his position as governor. He'd give the sheriff a chance to take King TenEyck into custody. When Chavez failed, he'd move against Crown immediately.

Youngbear couldn't see how a civil war was going to be averted. Neither Ludlow nor TenEyck was going to yield. It was like the old saw about an irresistible object meeting an immovable body. He had the sudden, uncomfortable feeling that he and Chavez were in between.

TenEyck slammed the door thunderously and turned. Senator Ingraham stepped out of his way, then followed him back into the living room. A fire was burning in the stone fireplace. The ceiling of the room was high, crossed by rough-hewn beams twelve inches square. Game heads decorated the walls. The floor was covered by a scattering of Indian rugs. There was a gun rack on one wall, holding more than a dozen rifles and shotguns. TenEyck walked over to the fireplace, spreading his hands to the flames as if they were cold. He growled, "All right. Say it and get it over with."

Ingraham said, "You're playing right into Ludlow's hands. He wants you to refuse to give Harvey up. He wants you to refuse to surrender yourself."

TenEyck turned his great, shaggy head. "And you think I ought to give him up? That I ought to give myself up?"

"If you give Harvey up, Ludlow won't be able to get a warrant charging you with harboring a fugitive."

"They'll take Harvey out of jail and string him up."

"How do you know that, King?"

"I know that son-of-a-bitch."

"I'm not so sure you do. All you can see is the hate between the two of you. What you can't see is the ambition in the man. I'm not saying he didn't love his daughter. I'm not saying he isn't grieving for her. But I am saying his political ambition overrides everything else in his life. He wants to be President, King. He wants to be Senator from Colorado and he thinks that's the steppingstone he needs."

"What's that got to do with giving Harvey up?"

"What I'm telling you is that he won't risk letting his men lynch Harvey."

TenEyck snorted. "You ever meet Sam Rork?"

"Can't say I have."

"Well, I know him. He used to work for me. He's as unpredictable as a rattlesnake. Ludlow might be able to control him part of the time, but I'm not going to bet Harvey's life he can control Rork all the time."

"Then you won't do it?"

TenEyck shook his head. "I'll fight him to a standstill. When I'm through with him, he won't be able to get elected dog catcher."

"I hoped . . ."

Unexpectedly TenEyck grinned. "That you could talk some sense into *me?* Not a chance, Arnold. I didn't build Crown by being reasonable. I didn't get you elected senator by being reasonable."

Ingraham's face flushed faintly and his eyes briefly flashed. TenEyck said soothingly, "No offense meant, Arnold. You've been a good senator. Nobody thinks I pull the strings."

Ingraham said bluntly, "You don't."

"That's what I said." There was a new edge to TenEyck's voice. "But don't get the idea you can get along without me because you can't."

The two men's glances locked. It was Ingraham's that fell away. He said, "I know what I owe you, King. Don't force a man to crawl."

TenEyck's manner abruptly changed. "What we both need right now is a goddam drink."

The tension between them relaxed. Ingraham said relievedly, "That's a good idea," and followed TenEyck toward the liquor cabinet.

12.

By the time Youngbear got back to town, the warrant charging King TenEyck with harboring a fugitive was already in the sheriff's hands. Governor Ludlow had taken Judge Montoya away from his supper and insisted he issue it immediately. He had also given the sheriff a formal warrant for the arrest of Harvey TenEyck, charging him with the murder of Mary Ludlow.

Chavez asked, "What'd TenEyck say when you asked him to give Harvey up?"

"He said no."

"Was that all he said?"

Youngbear shook his head. "He also said he was going to give his men orders to shoot to kill—State Police, Militia, whoever the governor sent out there."

"What'd Ingraham have to say?"

"He advised TenEyck to give Harvey up but it didn't do any good."

Chavez cursed disgustedly. "The hell of it is, I think Harvey *would* be safe in jail."

"Were you able to get a U.S. marshal and deputy to come down here?"

Chavez shook his head. "The marshal wouldn't believe that Governor Ludlow would instigate the lynching of a prisoner."

Out in front of the courthouse, an automobile backfired noisily. Youngbear went to the door and glanced outside. He didn't recognize the automobile drawn up outside, not did he recognize the man coming across the lawn, removing goggles and cap as he walked. The man was dressed in a business suit.

He opened the door, stopping when he saw Youngbear. "I'm Jonas McCracken, with the Denver *Post*."

Chavez said wearily, "Let him come in."

Youngbear stood aside and the reporter came in. He said, "We've been getting all kinds of stories, Sheriff, and some of them sound pretty wild. Maybe you can give me the straight of it."

Chavez said, "The governor's daughter was shot last night. She's dead."

"Got any leads?"

"We have a suspect," Chavez said.

"In jail? Can I talk to him?"

"He's not in custody. It's King TenEyck's son and he's out at TenEyck's ranch. I have warrants here for him and for King TenEyck that I'm about to go out and serve."

The reporter whistled. "Can I use your phone? And can I go with you when you go out to TenEyck's ranch?"

Chavez shrugged. "Go ahead. But be sure you call collect."

The reporter crossed the room to the phone. He cranked vigorously and yelled at the operator that he wanted the Denver *Post* in Denver. He gave her the number and waited impatiently. After several minutes, he began to shout into the phone the details of what was happening in Mesilla. Finished, he listened several more minutes. Then he said, "I'll call you as soon as I have anything new." He hung up.

Turning, he said, "My Oldsmobile is outside. I'll be glad to drive you out to Crown."

The sheriff hesitated, obviously aware of the time he might save by accepting McCracken's offer. At last he nodded. "All right. Let's go."

He looked at Youngbear. "Stay here and keep an eye on things. I ought to be back in a couple of hours at the most."

Jesse Youngbear nodded. Chavez went out with McCracken and Youngbear heard the car start, roar briefly, then chug away down the street.

Youngbear knew that serving the warrants, or trying to was only a formality. TenEyck would refuse to surrender either his son or himself, and Chavez wasn't fool enough to try taking either one of them by force.

But the formality of trying to serve the warrants and being formally refused would put the governor clearly in the right, both legally and morally, and would open the way for him to take whatever forceful measures he might decide upon. Youngbear figured he knew what they would be. A call-up of the Militia and an attack on Crown. With King TenEyck dead, nothing would stand between Ludlow and Arnold Ingraham's Senate seat.

A couple of times, he got up and paced back and forth across the office. Both times, he forced himself to sit down again. He was more nervous and apprehensive than he could ever remember being before. He felt as if he and Chavez were sitting on a box of dynamite, watching the lighted fuse burning closer to the inevitable explosion and unable to do anything about stopping it.

An hour and a half after leaving, Chavez walked into the office again. McCracken's Oldsmobile gave a roar at the curb and then chugged off down the street toward the Elkhorn Hotel.

Youngbear glanced at Chavez questioningly. Chavez shrugged. "It was predictable. He said he had no intention of surrendering either Harvey or himself."

"That's all Ludlow needs."

Chavez nodded. "McCracken's headed for the phone at the hotel to call in his story. He says it'll come out as an extra tomorrow morning. Ludlow will probably wait for the paper to come out but I figure we can look for him to attack Crown just as soon as he can get a large enough force of the Militia down here."

"Have you told Ludlow that TenEyck refused to surrender himself?"

"Huh-uh. Go down and do it now, will you?"

Youngbear got up and went outside. It was a warm night and there was a partial moon in the western sky.

The lobby of the hotel was still crowded with State Police. Youngbear didn't see the governor. He crossed to the lobby desk. Jim Oglethorp was on duty. Youngbear asked, "The governor in his room?"

Oglethorp nodded. "Number one."

"Thanks." Youngbear crossed the lobby and climbed the stairs. There was a uniformed state policeman on duty in front of what was pretentiously called the Presidential Suite. Youngbear said, "I want to see the governor."

The man nodded, turned, and knocked on the door. It opened and he said, "The sheriff's deputy wants to see the governor."

The door opened wider and Jesse went in. Ludlow was sitting in an ornate chair upholstered in red velvet. Youngbear said, "The sheriff tried to serve the warrants, Governor, but he was refused. He wanted me to tell you."

If he had expected Ludlow to be disappointed, he was wrong. The man smiled and nodded with satisfaction. Youngbear asked, "What are you going to do?"

Ludlow frowned. "Never mind, Deputy. Never mind."

Youngbear said, "I wouldn't advise you to break the law."

"Break it? I'm just going to see that it's upheld. That's my sworn duty as governor of this state."

Youngbear said drily, "And that means you're going to attack TenEyck's ranch."

"We will take enough men to Crown to insure the surrender of both King TenEyck and his son. I'll send Rork to the sheriff's office to pick up the warrants right away."

Youngbear knew there was no use discussing it further. The governor's mind was made up. This was part of his plan and it wasn't going to change.

He nodded curtly at the governor and withdrew from the suite. He went downstairs, crossed the lobby, and walked swiftly back to the courthouse. He reported to Chavez what Ludlow had said.

Chavez nodded. "He's probably already sent for a couple of companies of Militia. If he hasn't, he's doing it right now."

"How long do you figure it will take them to get down here?"

"Tomorrow afternoon."

"What are *you* going to do?"

Chavez got no opportunity to answer him. The door opened and Senator Ingraham came in. His face was tired and he wore a worried frown. He looked at Chavez. "I did the best I could, but it didn't do any good. He won't give Harvey up and he won't give himself up. I don't see how anyone can stop it now."

Chavez said, "You might still have a chance. Send a telegram to the President. Tell him we need three or four companies of Regular Army troops."

Ingraham nodded. "I'll try it but I'm not sure it will work. President Roosevelt is not going to want to interfere in state affairs. Particularly since he's going to be up for election in the fall."

Ingraham went out. Youngbear watched through the open door. He saw the senator drive away in his hired rig. He turned away from the door, frowning. Chavez asked, "What's the matter with you?"

Youngbear shrugged. "You don't suppose . . . ?"

"What?"

"Ludlow wouldn't dare tamper with a United States Senator. Or would he?"

"If you're worried, go ahead and follow Ingraham until he gets his wire sent."

Youngbear grinned. "Maybe I will." He hurried out and across the lawn to where his gray was tied. He untied the reins and mounted. Turning the horse, he trotted him toward the telegraph office in the depot at the lower end of the street.

Ingraham's buggy was halted in front of the depot. The tether weight was clipped to the horse's bridle. As Youngbear rode up, Ingraham came out of the telegraph office, accompanied by Rork and three patrolmen. Youngbear asked, "Is anything wrong, Senator?"

Ingraham glanced at him. Rork muttered something to the senator, something Youngbear couldn't hear. Ingraham said hastily, "Nothing's wrong, Deputy. Why do you ask?"

"Did you send your telegram?"

"Yes. Yes, of course."

Youngbear frowned. He strongly suspected that the senator was in custody. He also was aware that anything he might do could be dangerous, not only to himself but to the senator as well. Rork was scowling at him murderously, as if hoping he would start something.

Rork and Ingraham got into the senator's buggy and drove away. The other two state policemen followed the buggy on foot, not a difficult task since the buggy headed uptown at a pace no faster than a man could walk.

Frowning, Youngbear dismounted, tied his horse and went inside. The telegrapher glanced up. He was a new man, recently assigned to the office in Mesilla. Youngbear asked, "Did the senator just send a message to Washington?"

"I can't divulge . . ."

Youngbear's patience was wearing thin. He was nervous and edgy and tired of people refusing to co-operate with the law. He slammed the flat of his hand down on the counter so hard the telegrapher jumped. He said angrily, "I asked you a question and I want an answer!"

The telegrapher's voice was scared. "He wanted to send a telegram but Mr. Rork took it away from him as soon as he had it written out. He read it and tore it up. Then he and two of his men took the senator away."

"Where are the scraps?"

The telegrapher pointed to the cuspidor. Youngbear could see some of the scraps floating in it. He asked, "Any idea what was in the telegram?"

"No, sir. I never got a chance to look at it."

Youngbear nodded and went outside. He didn't need to piece the telegram together to know what it had contained. He untied his horse, mounted and rode toward the courthouse at a walk. He was worried and now he was beginning to feel scared. When a United States Senator wasn't safe, things were getting pretty bad.

13.

Ingraham's buggy was parked in front of the Elkhorn, but the senator was not in sight. Youngbear halted his horse a moment uncertainly. Sam Rork came out of the hotel. He glanced at Youngbear, scowled, then tramped along the walk toward the courthouse. Youngbear followed, pacing him.

Rork went into the sheriff's office. Youngbear tied his horse and followed. By the time he reached the door, Rork had concluded his business with the sheriff. He had the two warrants in his hand.

Youngbear stood aside reluctantly to let him pass. Chavez looked chagrined at having handed the warrants over to Rork. He glanced at Youngbear defensively.

Youngbear said, "The senator didn't get his telegram sent. Rork tore it up and threw the pieces into the spittoon. Then they went up to the hotel. I think Senator Ingraham's a prisoner."

Joe Chavez got up and began to pace back and forth. "I feel so goddam helpless!" he fumed. "I can't buck the governor of the state. Even if I tried, his State Police outnumber us."

"They won't hurt Ingraham."

"No, of course not. But they're pretty damn arrogant to even make him a prisoner."

"Mind if I go eat?"

"No. Go ahead."

Youngbear went out. He left his horse at the tie rail and walked downtown toward the Cowboy's Rest Saloon. For one thing, he wanted a beer with his supper. For another he wanted to see if Daisy Kyle had come to work tonight. He'd been too busy to go out to Daisy's house and fix the lock the way he'd promised.

He supposed he would ride out there with her tonight when she got off work and fix it for her then. He could at least put a bolt on the door so that it could be locked from inside the house. There was an old rusty bolt in a box in the basement of the courthouse that he could use.

He saw Daisy the minute he walked into the saloon. She caught his eye and smiled. He went to the bar, got a mug of beer and carried it to a table against the wall. Half a dozen men spoke to him and he returned their greetings absently. The mood in the place was subdued. He supposed everybody was concerned about the impending violence between the governor's State Police and TenEyck's men.

He drank about half his beer before Daisy could come to his table. She sat down across from him. Her smile was tired, and he could tell smiling hurt her bruised lips. She said, "I hear you beat Rork up."

He grinned self-consciously.

"I hear you did a pretty thorough job." Her color heightened and her glance held his softly and insistently. "Thanks."

It was Youngbear's turn to be embarrassed but his grin widened. "It was a pleasure. But I didn't get out to fix your door."

"You can ride out with me when I get off work."

"All right."

She got to her feet. "Are you having supper?"

"Uh-huh."

"I'll get it for you."

She hurried away. He wondered what dinner was to-night. Ordinarily they served only one dinner at the saloon. If you wanted variety you went someplace else.

He finished the beer, got up and went to the bar to have his mug refilled. He returned to his table, looked up and saw Daisy coming with his meal. She put it in front of him. She smelled nice and clean when she leaned close to him.

He said, "You shouldn't have come to town."

"Maybe not, but I'm not going to give Sam Rork the satisfaction of thinking he's got me scared." She saw someone beckoning for her, and left. Youngbear finished eating his supper and drank his beer. There had been a time when bartenders had refused to serve him, saying he was an Indian but it hadn't happened now for a long, long time. He supposed that meant they now thought of him as a white man rather than as an Indian. He grinned faintly at the thought.

He heard the pound of hoofs out in the street. Leaving his table he went to the door and looked out. Rork was galloping past, followed by twenty-five or thirty of the State Police.

Men crowded around Youngbear in the doorway. Some spilled past him into the street. All of them looked scared. All knew where Rork and his men were going. They had guessed what they were going to do.

Youngbear went back inside, glancing at the clock as he did. It was eight-thirty. He laid a quarter on the table, put on his hat and started for the door. Passing Daisy on the way, he asked, "What time?"

"Ten. I ought to be through by then."

"All right." He pushed through the crowd in front of the saloon. They were talking now, with suppressed excitement, wondering how King TenEyck would deal with Rork and his State Police.

Youngbear hurried toward the courthouse, wondering what Chavez would have to say.

As he galloped past, Rork saw Youngbear come to the door of the Cowboy's Rest. He scowled, but the scowl quickly disappeared. Nothing could spoil his mood of exhilaration tonight for very long.

The warrants were in the pocket of his shirt, but that was only a formality. King TenEyck wouldn't surrender either himself or his son. He figured he was above the law. He was about to discover that he was not.

Governor Ludlow had telegraphed for the State Militia. Two companies were on the way, or soon would be. They'd catch the eleven o'clock train out of Denver, along with their horses and a couple of pieces of artillery. They'd arrive in Mesilla around two in the morning.

Jonas McCracken's story would come out as an extra in the early morning hours. But before it hit the Denver streets, the war between Governor Ludlow and King TenEyck would be under way. After tonight, there could be no going back.

He held his horse at a steady trot until he was well clear of the town. After that, he kicked him into a lope and forced him to maintain that pace until he reached the gate across the road. Someone in town might try to ride out to Crown and warn TenEyck of his approach. He wanted to have his work done by the time TenEyck could react. TenEyck had three or four times as many men as he.

Once through the gate, he again forced his horse to lope. Shortly thereafter, he saw the lights of the first town on his right, the town where most of the families of TenEyck's married cowhands lived.

He left the road, angling toward it. There would have to be a pretense of searching the town for Harvey TenEyck, of course, to give everything an appearance of legality. What happened must, at least, appear to be an accident.

At the outskirts of the town, Rork drew his horse to a halt. He waved his men to right and left, keeping half a dozen of them with him. They spread through the town and Rork led his half dozen straight in along the road. Almost at once he could hear his men banging on doors, shouting at the occupants to submit to a search, that they had a warrant for Harvey TenEyck's arrest, and one for King TenEyck too.

Ahead, a man came out of his house with a shotgun in his hands. He was an elderly man, but dangerous with that shotgun in his hands. Rork shot him and saw him fall. The shotgun discharged into the air and Rork could hear the whistle of the charge.

Firing became general. Fearing the governor's wrath if more were killed, Rork bellowed, "Hold your fire! Or shoot over their heads! Pull back! Pull back!"

His men began to retreat, firing as they did. Another shotgun in the hands of one of the townspeople roared. The shot stung the horses and some of the men. The retreat became a rout. Three bodies now lay in the narrow, dusty road. All three had been defenders of the town.

Rork waited until his men were clear of the town. Then he shouted, "Burn it! Spread out and burn it!"

His men scattered around the town's perimeter, entering stables and empty shacks. Several moments elapsed before Rork saw the first of the tongues of flame, before he smelled the first smoke drifting toward him on a freshening wind out of the southwest.

His horse fidgeted nervously, frightened by the smell of smoke. He held the animal still. He couldn't help feeling apprehensive about what he had done. He remembered the governor's anger over the beating of

Daisy Kyle. Governor Ludlow hadn't told him to burn this town. He had only told him to serve the warrants if he could.

He could always say the old man with the shotgun had fired first. His men would back him up.

With that decided, he felt easier in his mind. Shacks and stables were now burning all around town. Flames blowing toward its center from the southwest had already caught other buildings in their path. At one spot on the far side, flames were shooting fifty feet into the air. Rork could hear the women's screams, the shouts of the boys and older men as they tried to organize some kind of fire brigade.

His men began to return, by twos and threes. Rork waited impatiently for the last of them. King TenEyck could see the flames from Crown, he thought. He'd be arriving soon.

The governor had said to avoid a confrontation with TenEyck's crew. Rork made a quick count of his men. All were back. He yelled, "Let's go!"

He spurred his horse and thundered away down the road, his men coming hard behind. Only when he reached the gate did he slow and let his lathered horse walk.

Glancing behind, he saw a red glow in the sky. The whole damn town must be burning now, he thought.

TenEyck and his men would stay to help fight the flames as long as there was hope of saving anything. That might be an hour or more. It could be longer than that. In the end, though, sometime before morning

TenEyck and his crew would descend on Mesilla. They would commit the ultimate act of lawlessness. They would attack the governor and his State Police.

Rork began to grin. Governor Ludlow had planned this very well. They could hold off TenEyck by forting up in the hotel. They could hold him off until the Militia arrived on the early morning train.

14.

Jesse Youngbear and Sheriff Joe Chavez were both at the courthouse when the red glow appeared in the southern sky. Youngbear saw it first and called the sheriff to the door. Neither spoke for a long time. Both knew what had caused the glow. Rork had fired the employees' town on Crown.

At last Chavez whistled softly. "Well, that does it," he breathed.

The glow was growing stronger in the sky. Youngbear said, "The whole damn town must be afire."

"And King TenEyck will be coming here just as soon as he gets the fire out."

Neither man could see much chance of stopping the coming conflict, but Chavez muttered, "Jesus, it seems like there ought to be something we could do!"

"I might try talking TenEyck out of it," Youngbear said doubtfully.

Chavez drew in a long, slow breath. "All right, go ahead. It probably won't do any good, but try to make him hold back at least until tomorrow. Tell him he's going to run head-on into the Militia if he don't. I'll go down to the Elkhorn and try to get past the guard they've got on Ingraham. If I can get him away from them, maybe Si Ferguson will drive him up the line to the next telegraph station at Adamsville. If a United States Senator tells Washington we need federal troops, maybe they'll believe."

Youngbear nodded and hurried to his horse. The sheriff went back inside to turn out the lights. Youngbear mounted and rode down the street. He dismounted in front of the Cowboy's Rest. There was a crowd on the sidewalk staring at the glowing sky. The men were talking in lowered voices, as if they were afraid of being overheard.

Youngbear went inside. Daisy was at one of the front windows looking out. He said, "Don't wait for me. I may not be back by the time you get off work."

"Where are you going?"

"Out there to see if I can't talk TenEyck out of coming after Rork."

"Jesse, be careful." There was fear for him in her voice.

He grinned. "I will." He wasn't worried too much about her door. She could prop something against it to hold it shut. And it wasn't likely that Rork was going to be thinking about Daisy Kyle tonight.

Chavez was just entering the hotel as Jesse mounted and rode southward out of town. He kicked the horse into a steady lope, holding his pace until he saw a body of horsemen approaching him.

He stopped his horse before they reached him and positioned himself in the middle of the road. Rork was at the head of the group of State Police. He reined his horse to a halt and scowled at Youngbear truculently, his face faintly illuminated by the half-moon in the western sky. "What the hell do you want, Deputy?"

"That your work?"

Rork said insolently, "An accident, Deputy. All we were doing was trying to serve the warrants the sheriff turned over to us."

"Did you think you'd find King TenEyck and Harvey *there?*"

Rork shrugged. "It was a chance."

Youngbear didn't know why he had bothered to talk with Rork. It had been a waste of breath. He reined his horse to the side of the road and Rork and his men went past, urging their horses to a trot.

Youngbear rode on, went through the gate and galloped across country toward the still-burning cluster of houses and other buildings where most of TenEyck's employees lived with their families. He hoped the loss of life had not been heavy but he knew it was too much to expect that no one had been killed.

King TenEyck and at least two hundred people were clustered on the near side of the burning town. They were almost a quarter mile away from it but even at this distance the heat was almost unbearable. Youngbear forced his reluctant horse to where TenEyck stood, then dismounted from the prancing animal.

TenEyck's eyes were red from the glow of the flames. His face was an ugly mask of rage. He growled, "You get back to town, Deputy, and tell Joe Chavez he'd better go fishin' for a couple of days. I've got some snakes to kill and I don't want him in the way."

Youngbear said, "That's what I came out about. What do you think Ludlow and Rork expect you to do as soon as you get this fire out?"

"If they expect me to bring my men to town, they're right. I'm going to wipe out every goddam one of those thugs that Ludlow calls his State Police."

Youngbear asked, "What time is it?"

TenEyck pulled an ornate gold watch from his pocket and flipped open the hunting case. "After ten. Why?"

"Ludlow has got several companies of Militia coming on the train, along with horses and probably a couple of pieces of artillery. They'll get in at two, or maybe a little before."

"Then by God, we'll get our work done before they come."

"Ludlow will be holed up in the Elkhorn. His men will be shooting down at you. You can't take the hotel in a couple or three hours and you damn well know you can't."

"Then we'll burn 'em out, just the way they burned us out."

Youngbear felt the futility of further talk. He asked, "How many were hurt out here?"

❧ "Three killed. Two kids burned pretty bad. And the rest of these people lost every damn thing they had in the world."

Jesse said, "I'm sorry, Mr. TenEyck. But burning the town of Mesilla isn't going to bring their possessions back. There's got to be a better way."

"Go talk to the governor. Let that son-of-a-bitch show you a better way. He's the one who started this."

"Is he? If you'd given Harvey up, none of this would have happened."

"And Harvey would be dead, strung up without a trail."

"You won't change your mind?"

"No."

"Will you at least wait until you hear from me? The sheriff was going to try and get Senator Ingraham away from the hotel and get Si Ferguson to drive him to the telegraph station at Adamsville." He knew before the words were out that he'd revealed something that should not have been revealed. TenEyck asked angrily, "What the hell are you talking about? Why can't he send a telegram from the station in Mesilla? And what do you mean, 'try and get him away from the hotel'?"

Youngbear knew that now he might as well tell TenEyck the truth. He said, "Chavez got the senator to try and send a telegram to Washington requesting Regular Army troops. Rork stopped him and tore up the telegram. Ingraham is at the hotel, guarded by the State Police."

"Why those dirty bastards! This time they've gone too far!" He glowered at Youngbear.

Youngbear said, "Give Joe Chavez a chance to get the senator out of the hotel. If he's still there when you attack, he could get killed."

TenEyck nodded reluctantly. "All right. I'll give you an hour. If I haven't heard from you by then, I'm coming in."

The flames were dying in the blazing village as more and more of the burnable materials were consumed. A roof fell in, causing a pillar of sparks to ascend on the overheated air. Youngbear mounted and rode back toward town, holding his horse to a walk until he was out of TenEyck's sight. Then he kicked the animal into a steady, mile-eating lope.

As Joe Chavez went into the Elkhorn Hotel, he turned his head and saw his deputy, Jesse Youngbear, riding toward the lower end of town. He had a gray certainty that Youngbear wasn't going to be able to talk Ten-Eyck out of anything. He was equally sure he wasn't going to be able to get Senator Ingraham away from the guards Ludlow had placed over him.

Chavez had been sheriff of Mesilla county for nearly twelve years now and in all that time he had never felt as helpless as he did tonight. He had never encountered a situation with which he felt unable to cope. He had pursued horse thieves, bank robbers, and killers with no doubts about his own competence or about the final outcome of the chase. He had jailed drunks who were shooting up the town and threatening to kill him if he tried disarming them. Looking back, he thought he had been a good sheriff. He had served the people well.

Where, then, had he failed last night and today? What had he done wrong? He couldn't put his finger on it but he knew that somehow he had permitted the situation in Mesilla to get out of hand.

It was now like a locomotive on a downgrade traveling at full throttle with the engineer and fireman both dead. There seemed to be no stopping it. And the destruction it promised was truly appalling. Rork and his men, when they got back, would take refuge in the hotel. King TenEyck, once the fire had been controlled, would bring his men into town and lay siege to the hotel. A lot of innocent people were going to be hurt, perhaps some even killed. A lot of property was going to be destroyed. All over Harvey TenEyck. Chavez shook his head. No. Harvey was only the excuse. What had really caused the trouble was the bitter, long-smoldering hatred between King TenEyck and Governor Ludlow. The long-postponed showdown had finally arrived.

He stepped into the Elkhorn lobby. Electric chandeliers burned overhead. The place was singularly empty. Ronny Lort, the night clerk, was behind the desk. McCracken, the newspaper reporter from the Denver *Post*, sat on a leather-covered sofa reading a newspaper. He lowered it enough to watch the sheriff over the top of it but he made no sign of recognition nor did he get up.

Chavez crossed to the desk. "Where's the governor?"

"Up in his room, Sheriff."

"And Senator Ingraham?"

The clerk looked blank. Chavez said softly, "Don't play dumb, Ronny. I'll be here when Governor Ludlow and his State Police are only a memory."

Ronny Lort said, "He's in seven, Sheriff. There's three men guarding him."

Chavez said, "I'm going through the kitchen and I'm going to come up the back stairs. Seven is right at the head of those stairs, isn't it?"

"Yes, sir."

"I want you to give me exactly five minutes. Then I want you to come upstairs with a pitcher of water and a tray of glasses. At the head of the lobby stairs, I want you to stumble and drop the tray. It ought to make enough racket to get the guards' attention for a minute or two, and that's all I'll need."

Ronny Lort's face lost color and he licked his lips. Chavez said reassuringly, "It's all right, Ronny. Nobody is going to blame you and there's no danger in what you're going to do."

"No, sir." But Ronny didn't sound convinced.

Chavez headed toward the hall that led to the kitchen in the rear of the hotel. Turning his head he said, "Five minutes, Ronny. Don't let me down."

Ronny's face had no color left in it. Chavez hurried along the hall and into the kitchen beyond. Two Mexican women were on their hands and knees, scrubbing the white tile kitchen floor. Chavez spoke to them in Spanish, walked apologetically on tiptoe where they had finished scrubbing and went through the other door to the stairway leading up to the second floor.

At the foot of it he paused, listening. He heard nothing. Cautiously he began his ascent, keeping his glance on the lighted area at the head of the stairs, easing his weight down carefully on each step so that, if the step started to squeak he could raise his foot again before the squeak was loud enough to be heard by the men at the head of the stairs.

He didn't bother looking at his watch. It would have been too dark to see it anyway. He supposed two or three minutes had passed since he had left Ronny Lort.

Halfway up, a stair tread squeaked. Quickly he raised his foot and stood there, hand on gun, one foot raised. Like a goddam stork, he thought to himself, grinning in the darkness. He put the foot down two steps above and eased himself on up.

A man said something in the hall at the head of the stairs but he couldn't make out what it was. Seconds later, he heard the crash of water pitcher and glasses as Ronny, at least two minutes ahead of schedule, dropped them at the head of the lobby stairs.

Chavez took the remaining stairs two at a time. His gun was drawn, the hammer back. A single dim light burned in the hall in front of room seven. By this light he saw the shapes of two blue-clad State Police. Both were facing away from him. The door of room seven was ajar and a shaft of light from it fell on the wall immediately opposite.

Chavez yelled, "Hold it, you two! Right where you

are!" To Ronny, beyond, he yelled, "Get back down those stairs, kid! Move!"

Ronny disappeared. Chavez heard him rolling down the lobby stairs, bumping each time he hit.

The two in front of room seven froze when Chavez yelled at them. Chavez said, "It's the sheriff, boys. Just drop your guns. Nice and easy now."

One of them dived into the room. The door slammed open, flooding the hall momentarily with light. Chavez cursed beneath his breath. Three guards, Ronny had said. And two of them were now inside the room.

The voice of Senator Ingraham yelled something, but it was cut off abruptly as though a hand had been clapped over his mouth. Inside the room, one of the guards shouted, "Clocker! Down!"

The man in the hall dropped flat. Instantly the other man jumped out of room seven into the hall. He was facing the sheriff as he did and in his hands he held a sawed-off shotgun. Its barrel looked, in that split second, like a cannon's bore.

Chavez saw the flame burst from the muzzle. Something hit him in the chest, something like the kick of a mule. He was driven back and felt himself rolling over and over down the back stairs. He kept on rolling, through the door and into the kitchen where the two Mexican women still were down on their knees.

They saw him, saw the mass of scarlet where his chest had been. One of them fainted. The other stood up and stared down at him and screamed and screamed as though she would never stop.

Chavez felt shock—and he felt unbelief. He was dying, and knew it, and that is always hard for any man to believe.

Then the light was gone. The burning in his chest was no more. He didn't see the two blue-uniformed men who came down the back stairs and stood in the kitchen door looking down at him. He didn't see Ronny Lort's white, stricken face in the other door and he didn't see the face of McCracken appear momentarily behind Ronny Lort and then disappear again.

He had long ago accepted the probability that this was the way he was going to die, so it should have come as no surprise. Yet death, when it comes quickly and violently, is always a surprise.

15.

❦ The reporter, McCracken, ran through the lobby toward the door opening onto the street. He had witnessed the murder of a law officer and he had seen the face of the killer. He had seen the gun smoking in his hands.

He didn't know whether the two had seen him or not. He had foolishly crossed the lobby behind the clerk, Ronny Lort, when he heard the screams of the Mexican scrubwoman. He had foolishly peered over Ronny's shoulder through the partially opened door.

Now all he could think was that he had to get away. The killer and his accomplice would eliminate all witnesses if they could. The clerk, Ronny Lort, was doomed because they had most certainly seen his face. The Mexican scrubwomen were as good as dead. McCracken knew Governor Ludlow's State Police. He knew they were little more than thugs in uniforms.

Outside, he turned right and hurried down the darkened street. Before he stepped into the arc light's aura, he glanced nervously behind to see if anyone was following. He wished that he was back in the city room of the *Post*. He wished he'd never heard of Mary Ludlow, or of the town of Mesilla.

He was shaking and his body was bathed with clammy sweat. Where could he go? How was he going to get away? He couldn't take the train because it would involve waiting here in Mesilla for it to arrive. He couldn't go to the livery stable for a horse. They might be watching for him there. And he didn't dare try for his car, still parked in front of the courthouse. It made enough racket when it was started to wake the dead.

Beyond the intersection and the glare of the arc light, he stopped. He had to get out of town and he had to get out right away.

A buggy creaked toward him, the horse trotting, making a *clop clop* sound with his hoofs. A woman was driving, and as the buggy passed under the arc light, McCracken recognized the girl who worked in the Cowboy's Rest Saloon.

He waited until the buggy was almost abreast. Then he stepped into the street and stopped the horse by seizing his bridle. The horse stood placidly enough and the woman made no sound except for her swiftly indrawn breath. When she spoke, her voice was calm, if strained with fright. "What do you want?"

"Don't be afraid, ma'am. My name's McCracken. I'm a reporter for the *Post*." He paused and realized he was breathing fast. His chest was as constricted as though he had been running. The words rushed out, "I just saw two of Ludlow's State Police murder the sheriff. I

don't know whether they know I saw it or not, but I
don't intend to take any chances. I've got to get out of
town, ma'am, and hide. I thought maybe I could ride a
ways with you."

"They killed Joe Chavez?" Her voice was incredulous,
then filled with a kind of quiet terror. "What about
Jesse Youngbear, his deputy?"

"He wasn't with the sheriff, ma'am."

"Thank God!" she breathed.

McCracken said, "Ma'am?"

Her shocked voice said, "Get in. Get in."

He climbed into the buggy and the horse trotted on
down the silent street. Looking back, McCracken saw
no one in front of the hotel. Nothing appeared to be
unusual about the scene. He began to breathe more
easily. Perhaps they hadn't seen him after all. Perhaps . . .

But he didn't feel reassured. They would know he
couldn't escape from them. They might just be busy
disposing of the sheriff's body, taking care that neither
Ronny Lort, the clerk, nor the Mexican scrubwomen
lived to talk about what they had seen.

And what about Senator Ingraham? he wondered.
Hadn't the senator seen the murder? Wouldn't they dis-
pose of Ingraham as ruthlessly as they disposed of the
other witnesses?

He was appalled—at what was happening here in Mesilla, at the chain of violent events Harvey TenEyck's
murder of Mary Ludlow had set in motion. Harvey's
cowardice in failing to carry out his end of the suicide

pact had already cost Sheriff Chavez his life. Before the night was over, three more would die for Harvey's cowardice. And that was only the beginning. King TenEyck and the governor still had not locked horns. When they did . . .

His reporter's news gathering instinct warred in McCracken with his terror, with his fear for his life. Here he was, sitting on the biggest story of his career, perhaps the biggest story that would ever come his way. And he didn't dare stay in town and see it played out to the end. He turned to Daisy Kyle and asked, "You got a phone out at your place?"

She had turned the buggy off the main road. Behind and to their right was the Jaramillo shack where the murder had taken place.

"No. Outside of town, TenEyck's Crown has the only phone."

"How far is that?"

"Ten miles. That way." She pointed toward the red glow in the southern sky.

He asked, "What's that glow?" It was the first time he had noticed it, so preoccupied had he been with his own fear.

"Fire. There's a town between here and Crown headquarters, where the families of Crown's employees live. The men in the saloon figured Rork had set fire to that town."

McCracken whistled softly. This story was big but it was getting bigger all the time. He looked back toward the main road that led to Crown. If Rork and his

State Police had fired the town on TenEyck's ranch, they'd be returning before very long. They'd probably be using the road. But if he could walk, across country to Crown headquarters . . . Not only would he be safe but a telephone would be available to him. He would be able to call his story in to the *Post*.

He said quickly, "Stop the buggy. I want to get out."

She pulled the buggy horse to a halt. "Where are you going? I thought . . ."

"I'm going to try walking across country to Crown ranch."

"What about Sam Rork and his men?"

"I figure they'll be staying on the road."

She made an almost imperceptible shrug. He couldn't see her face. The buggy top shaded it from the soft glow of the moon. He climbed out of the buggy. "Thanks, ma'am."

She said, "Jesse must be someplace between here and there. He said he was going to try talking Mr. TenEyck out of coming after Rork. When you told me the sheriff was dead, I was afraid that maybe he'd come back, or changed his mind about going or something. I thought he might have been with the sheriff . . ." Her voice trailed off.

McCracken said, "If you don't mind, don't tell anybody you've seen me."

"I won't." He could tell she was still profoundly shocked by the news of the sheriff's death. She clucked to the horse and drove away. McCracken stared after her only a moment before turning toward the red glow, now beginning to fade in the southern sky.

He began to walk swiftly toward it. There was enough moonlight to see the ground, to avoid gullies and brush clumps and rocks. For the first time since witnessing the sheriff's murder he felt secure.

He was about a quarter mile from the road, and he saw Rork and his State Police ride by. Half an hour later, he saw a lone horseman on the road, also heading back toward town. He didn't know it was Youngbear but he supposed it was. He didn't run toward the road and he didn't try shouting at the solitary rider. He was too fearful it might be one of Ludlow's men.

He had almost reached the smoldering remains of the burned-out town when he saw an even larger group of men riding toward the town. They seemed in no great hurry and were riding at a walk.

He knew these could only be King TenEyck's men. He began to run toward the road. He fell down several times, but each time he got up and ran again. At last he was close enough to shout at them, close enough for his shouts to be heard. They stopped. A couple of them left the road and came to where he stood, panting and sweating heavily. One of them asked, "Who the hell are you?"

He managed to say, "Jonas McCracken. I'm a reporter for the Denver *Post*. The sheriff's been murdered. I saw it and I figured they'd try to get rid of me."

One of the men said, "You better come tell that to

the boss, mister. Here. I'll give you a stirrup and you can swing up behind me."

The man pulled a boot out of his left stirrup. McCracken put a foot into it. The rider gave him a vigorous pull up, and he settled onto the horse's rump behind the man.

They rode quickly to the road, and stopped in front of a towering bull-shouldered man with hair like a lion's mane. McCracken recognized him from pictures he had seen as King TenEyck. The rider said, "He says his name is McCracken, boss. Claims he's a reporter for the *Post*."

"What the hell is he doing away out here?"

"Says the sheriff's dead. Murdered."

"Jesus Christ!" TenEyck's voice was shocked. "Who did it?"

The cowboy let McCracken speak for himself this time. McCracken said, "Ludlow's State Police. They had Senator Ingraham in a room upstairs under guard. The sheriff tried to get him away from them and they killed him. I saw it and I figured they saw me. I knew they'd have to get rid of the witnesses if they could."

"Who else saw it?"

"The clerk. I think his name is Ronny Lort. Two Mexican scrubwomen were in the kitchen when the sheriff's body came rolling down the stairs."

TenEyck asked, "Where you going, mister? What do you want to do? I can send a man back to the ranch with you."

For an instant Jonas McCracken hesitated. His reporter's instinct won out over his fear. What could happened to him surrounded by TenEyck's men? He said, "If it's all the same to you, I'd like to go back to town."

TenEyck grunted his assent. He shouted, "All right, let's go! The sheriff couldn't do anything! Maybe, by God, we can!"

16.

Jesse Youngbear reached town well ahead of King Ten-
Eyck's men. There were a couple of members of the
State Police standing in front of the Elkhorn Hotel.
All the second-floor front windows of the hotel were
dark and Youngbear supposed that troopers with rifles
were stationed in them, waiting for TenEyck to arrive.

He rode past the hotel and went straight to the courthouse. The sheriff's office was dark. Seeing it so put a
peculiar feeling of uneasiness in his mind. He wondered
where Joe Chavez could be.

He tied his horse, crossed the lawn and went into the
office. He lighted the lamp and looked beside it for a
note. There was none. Frowning, he paced nervously
back and forth for several minutes. At last he blew out
the lamp and went outside.

He stood indecisively in front of the door. TenEyck
had given him an hour. After that he'd be coming in,
though he probably wouldn't try attacking the hotel

until dawn. He wondered how TenEyck planned to cope with the State Militia.

Deciding that the best place to begin looking for the sheriff was where he'd seen him last, he mounted his horse and rode down the street to the hotel. He dismounted and tied, then passed between the two state troopers and went into the lobby.

No clerk was on duty. Rork stood in the middle of the huge room. His face looked like it had been through a meat grinder. His lips were smashed and puffy, scabbed where they had been cut. His nose was swelled almost twice its normal size and one of his eyes was black and swelled partly shut. The scratches of Daisy's fingernails still marked his cheek from forehead to jawline. His front teeth were gone.

He scowled at Youngbear, his eyes murderous. "What the hell do you want?"

"I'm looking for the sheriff. Last I saw of him, he was coming here."

There was the slightest hesitation in Rork, but when he answered, his words were positive enough. "He ain't here and he ain't been here, at least not since I got back."

"I want to see Senator Ingraham."

"You can't."

"Are you telling me what I can't do?"

"I'm telling you." Rork nodded at a couple of his men. They shifted their rifles until they were pointing straight at the deputy.

Youngbear said, "They wouldn't shoot."

Rork said, "Try them."

Youngbear looked steadily into Rork's eyes a moment. He glanced at the faces of each of the men whose rifles were trained on him. He knew suddenly that this was a confrontation he couldn't win. They *would* shoot if he tried going up the stairs to see the senator. He shrugged. "All right. But how long do you think you can get away with keeping a U.S. senator prisoner?"

"Long enough."

Youngbear turned and left the hotel. Walking away from Rork and his two men, his back ached with the expectation of a bullet striking it. Rork was capable of shooting him in the back but he doubted if Rork would do it in front of witnesses.

Outside, he untied his horse and swung to the animal's back. He rode quickly away, heading down the street toward the depot and the telegraph office at its lower end. He was beginning to feel genuinely worried about Joe Chavez. His inability to find the sheriff puzzled him.

The depot was dark. There wasn't even a light in the telegraph office. Youngbear circled the building, frowning, then headed back uptown again. Nervously he glanced southward toward TenEyck's ranch.

Somebody ought to be able to tell him where Chavez had gone. He rode up the street to the Cowboy's Rest, but found it closed as well. Back to the courthouse, only to discover it was as dark as he had left it a few minutes before.

For the first time, he put his doubts into words, if

only in his mind. Had they done something to Joe Chavez? Had they taken him prisoner the way they had the senator?

Forcing his horse to trot, he rode down the street to the hotel corner, cut into the side street and when he reached the alley, turned into it. He knew he made a good target on the back of his horse if anyone wanted to take a shot at him, but as jumpy as the state troopers were about TenEyck, it might be better to ride down the alley openly than to skulk down it afoot.

Behind the hotel, his horse shied suddenly. He tried to quiet the animal, but the horse would not be controlled. Something had frightened him, something either in or beside a small shed across the alley from the back door of the hotel.

Youngbear dismounted quickly and tied the horse to the fence. Cautiously he walked in the direction the horse's ears had been pricked. His foot encountered something yielding and he fell to his knees, sprawling out flat over a body lying on the ground.

He scrambled to his feet and fumbled for a match. The moon was low in the sky and the body was in shadow. He found a match and struck it on the fence, knowing even before he looked what he was going to find.

The body was that of Joe Chavez. The whole front of his shirt was a welter of shredded flesh and clotted blood. A shotgun blast at close range, Youngbear thought numbly. Joe probably hadn't known what hit him.

The match burned his fingers and he struck another

ν one. The sheriff's eyes were closed. His face looked
peaceful. Youngbear realized numbly that tears were
spilling from his eyes. His throat felt raw and tight.
He'd never thought about it much until now, but the
sheriff had been like a father to him. He couldn't remember his own father, who had died when he was
four. Chavez had filled an aching void, almost from the
time young Jesse's mother had brought him to Mesilla
to live.

Anger grew in him like a tiny flame in dry grass.
Anger drove away his tears and made a different kind of
tightness in his chest. He promised himself that he
would find the man who had done this and that he
would see him hanged.

He lifted Joe Chavez's body carefully and walked
down the alley to its end. He headed straight for
Phinney's place.

There were no lights inside, so he carried the sheriff's
body on up to the courthouse. He was sweating from
head to foot from exertion when he arrived. He managed to get the door open and carried the sheriff inside,
wondering if he would make it to the office cot before
he fell.

He did and he laid Chavez's body down. He straightened, breathing hard and fast. He went to the washbasin
and splashed water into his face. He took a long, cold
drink. He still couldn't believe that Chavez was dead.
It was so incredible, so utterly unbelievable.

Hands shaking, he lighted the office lamp. He crossed
to the cot and for a moment stood looking down, the

same tightness once more coming to his throat. Then he crossed to the office phone.

He had to crank several times before Myrtle answered. He said harshly, "Get Albert Phinney. Keep ringing until you wake him up."

The phone rang interminably, but at last Phinney's sleepy voice answered it. Youngbear said, "This is Jesse Youngbear. The sheriff's been killed. I'm at the courthouse with his body. I want you to come right down."

There was a silence at the other end of the line. Youngbear said, "Mr. Phinney?"

"I'll be right there, Jesse. Fifteen minutes."

Jesse hung up. He was certain in his own mind that Chavez had been killed inside the hotel. He knew as surely the sheriff had been killed by Ludlow's State Police.

He also knew that if he went into the hotel looking for the killers or for witnesses, he'd never come out of it alive. They had killed the sheriff. They might have killed Ronny Lort, the clerk. That may have been why he hadn't been in the lobby behind the desk. And having killed the sheriff and possibly some witnesses, they wouldn't hesitate about killing the sheriff's deputy.

But there had to be some way of discovering who the killers were. Maybe, he thought, Senator Ingraham would know.

Frowning, he admitted to himself that if Senator Ingraham did know, if he had witnessed the shooting of Chavez, then he was in mortal danger himself, despite the fact that he was a U.S. senator. It would be simple enough for Ludlow and Rork to claim he had been shot accidentally during TenEyck's dawn attack on the hotel.

Youngbear began to pace nervously back and forth. He felt alone and helpless. Chavez had always been on hand to tell him what to do. Now Chavez was gone and he was on his own. He was moreover, in a situation which even the sheriff had admitted he didn't know how to control.

He heard hoofs in the street. He went to the door. Phinney's hearse was drawing to a halt outside. Phinney clipped a tether weight to the near horse's bridle, then opened the hearse doors wide. He took out a stretcher and came across the lawn carrying it.

Coming in, he glanced at the sheriff's body. He said feelingly, "God, I'm sorry, Jesse! Do you know who . . . ?"

Jesse said, "Ludlow's bunch. I don't know which one yet, but before I'm through I will."

"Where'd you find him?"

"In the alley back of the hotel. Dumped out there like so much garbage. The sons-of-bitches!"

Phinney placed the stretcher beside the office cot. Youngbear helped him lift the sheriff's body onto it. Afterward he lifted one end of the stretcher while Phinney lifted the other. They carried Chavez's body out to the hearse and carefully placed it inside.

Phinney closed the doors. He turned to Jesse. "When do you want to bury him?"

"I don't know. Day after tomorrow, I suppose."

Again Phinney said, "I'm sorry."

• "Thanks." Jesse Youngbear turned away hastily and hurried to the courthouse door. He went in, blew out the lamp, then came back out again. He walked downtown, turned at the hotel corner and then hurried down the alley toward the place he had tied his horse. He'd go over the ground behind the hotel thoroughly tomorrow when it was light. There was no use trying to do it by lantern light. Besides, with a lantern he'd make too good a target for the men inside the hotel.

Rork wanted him dead; there was little doubt of that. And Rork was capable of killing him from ambush if he thought there was no other way.

He untied his horse, mounted, and returned the way he had come. At the corner beside the hotel, he halted, staring toward the south. TenEyck would be arriving soon, if he wasn't already here. But TenEyck would have more sense than to ride in openly and try a frontal assault upon the Elkhorn Hotel. That would be too costly. Ludlow's men would cut his men down with little loss to themselves.

Jesse crossed Main and rode to the street beyond. Turning here, he rode south again, not returning to Main Street until he reached the railroad tracks.

He took his watch from his pocket and, holding it so that the moonlight shone on it, saw that it was one o'clock. A voice came from the shadows . . . "Youngbear?"

"Uh-huh."

King TenEyck rode from behind the depot, accompanied by half a dozen men. He said, "I heard about the sheriff, Jesse. I'm sorry."

"How'd you hear?"

"Mr. McCracken. He saw it. Or at least he saw the sheriff come rolling down the stairs. And he saw the killer with his gun smoking in his hands."

Jesse said, "McCracken?"

"Yeah." A figure detached itself from the others and rode forward. Youngbear asked, "You saw who it was?"

"I sure did."

"And you can identify him?"

"Yes, sir."

TenEyck said, "I suppose they're waiting up there for us."

"Uh-huh."

"And the Militia is coming in on the train at two?"

"Uh-huh."

"Where do you stand, Deputy?"

Youngbear frowned at the bulky figure of King Ten-Eyck. He said, "I want Harvey for the murder of Mary Ludlow. I want the sheriff's killer and I want to keep the peace if that is possible. Just because one of them killed the sheriff, don't think I'm going to sanction civil war."

"Whether you want it or not, that's what you're going to have the minute the State Militia gets off the train."

With growing uneasiness, Jesse admitted to himself that what King TenEyck said was true.

17.

From behind the depot, a man yelled, "Hey, boss!"

TenEyck turned. Dan Malloy, foreman of Crown, came hurrying across the platform. "There's a gas-powered handcar over here in back of the station. If we got going now, we could get ten or fifteen miles up the track before we met the train."

TenEyck asked, "And run the handcar into it?"

"Huh-uh. I was thinking about dynamiting the track. If we could do that and stop the train around ten miles north of here—why hell, the Militia probably couldn't get here until well after daylight. I doubt if they can unload their horses without a chute or some kind of ramp, and it'd take a while to rig something up."

"Where are you going to get the dynamite?"

"There's a storage shed a hundred yards down the track. It's locked, but . . ."

TenEyck said, "Get going."

Malloy hurried away, calling for some of the men to help. Others manhandled the handcar onto the track.

One of them cranked the engine. It coughed a couple of times, then started with a roar. Youngbear said, "I'm going along."

"What for?"

"I want to make damn sure they don't wreck the train."

"You don't think I'd let them wreck a train, do you?"

"I think you would. If it suited you."

TenEyck shrugged. "Go ahead."

Youngbear tied his horse. He ran to the little handcar and jumped aboard. One of the men drove the car up the track to the dynamite shed. Dan Malloy and the others carried out half a dozen boxes of dynamite, fuse, and caps, and put them on the car. Malloy got aboard and yelled above the engine's noise, "Let's go!"

The handcar chugged away. Malloy noticed Youngbear and yelled, "What are you doing here?"

Youngbear yelled back, "Just making sure you don't wreck that train!"

Malloy shrugged. He sat down on the edge of the car, letting his feet dangle over the side. The lights of Mesilla faded into the darkness and disappeared.

The car must be going twenty miles an hour, Youngbear thought. They would probably have time to go a dozen miles before they'd have to stop and set the charges on the track.

He didn't worry about leaving Mesilla. He doubted if TenEyck would attack the hotel anyway until it got light enough to see. And even if TenEyck did attack sooner, his presence in town wouldn't change anything.

He couldn't stop TenEyck from doing what he wanted
to any more than he could control the governor and his
State Police.

He sat down beside Malloy, letting his feet dangle
over the side of the car. Malloy said, "I'm sorry about
the sheriff, Jesse."

Youngbear didn't answer him. It was still hard for
him to believe that Joe Chavez was dead. He was still
numb from the shock of it.

The engine chugged on steadily, making conversation
difficult. The air was chill. Jesse began to shiver in spite
of himself. He wondered what time it was but he knew
it would be useless trying to see his watch. The moon
had disappeared behind a bank of clouds.

It was certainly going to help matters if Malloy
succeeded in halting the train ten miles out of town.
It would at least keep the Militia away. It would keep the
trouble from getting any worse even if it wouldn't keep
TenEyck and Governor Ludlow apart.

Suddenly Youngbear saw a gleam of hope. If he could
get out to Crown before TenEyck began his attack on
the hotel at dawn . . . If he could capture Harvey
TenEyck and bring him in to jail . . .

That would take the wind out of Governor Ludlow's
sails. He'd have nothing left to fight about, particularly
since he was badly in the wrong for letting Rork and
his men burn the employees' town on Crown.

Harvey's capture wouldn't necessarily make TenEyck
give up his plan to attack the hotel but it might give
him something more important to think about. Like

guarding the jail to see that nobody tried to break Harvey out and string him up.

Youngbear wished now that he hadn't come along with Malloy and the others. He wished he had stayed in town. Still, he consoled himself, there should be enough time to do what he planned when he got back. The train would be stopped well before two o'clock. The handcar could surely make it back to town by two-thirty or three. That would give him plenty of time to ride out to Crown, take Harvey prisoner and return him to town.

It was almost impossible to guess time, but Youngbear knew the landmarks. He knew the butte that towered west of the tracks eight miles north of town. He knew the trestle across a dry wash a couple of miles farther on.

This was where Malloy ordered the handcar stopped. Short of the dry wash. Short by fifty yards.

The men piled off, each seizing a case of dynamite and carrying it to the edge of the wash. Youngbear said, "Better send someone up the track to flag down the train. There ought to be lanterns in that tool box on the handcar."

Malloy ordered two of the men to break open the tool box, get lanterns and walk up the track to halt the train. Youngbear watched them, relieved when they found two lanterns, one with clear glass and one with red. They lighted them, then walked across the trestle and headed north along the track.

Malloy used no particular finesse in planting the dynamite. He just opened the boxes and piled them on the

trestle in the middle of the wash. He unwrapped a
dozen sticks, molded them into a ball and with his teeth
crimped a cap onto a six-foot length of fuse. He pushed
the cap down into the ball of dynamite and placed it
on top of the piled-up boxes. He led the fuse out away
from the boxes and frayed its end. Then yelled at Youngbear and his men, "Get back to the handcar! Run it
toward town a couple of hundred yards!"

Youngbear and the men got on and one of the men
drove it back toward town. He didn't stop until the
trestle was three hundred yards away. Someone asked,
"What about Malloy?"

"Don't worry about Malloy. He'll be all right."

The trestle was too far away for Youngbear to see the
flare of the match, or that of the fuse. But he saw the
monstrous flash of the explosion. Its concussion, late
coming by what seemed like almost half a minute,
beat at his ears as if trying to rupture their drums.
Debris soared into the air. For almost a minute afterward it rained to the ground.

In the flash of the explosion, Youngbear had seen
Malloy running toward them. Almost immediately following the explosion, he heard the distant, mournful
whistle of the train.

Its headlight came into sight beyond the wrecked
trestle, moving noticeably with a wide curve of the track.
Slowly, deliberately then, it stopped. Youngbear could
see the lanterns waving beside the track. Someone
said, "Hadn't we better get the hell out of here?"

"And make Frank and Will walk back to town? Huh-
uh. We'll wait for them."

Then minutes dragged. Then men fidgeted, straining
their eyes into the darkness uneasily. There were two
or three companies of Militia aboard the train, and they
didn't fancy being shot at by that many men. Malloy,
Frank, and Will finally materialized out of the darkness.
All three were breathing fast.

Malloy said urgently, "Get going!"

The engine roared as whoever was driving advanced
the throttle. A sudden volley of rifle fire crackled from
the direction of the train. Youngbear could see the
muzzle flashes but over the engine's racket he couldn't
hear the reports.

They were shooting at the noise and there wasn't
much chance of their bullets hitting anything, but the
men aboard the handcar couldn't help ducking anyway.
It was instinctive.

A bullet clanged against metal someplace on the
handcar and ricocheted away, whining, into the darkness. The handcar was going at full speed now, the
breaks in the rails clicking rapidly beneath its wheels.
The shooting from the train stopped.

Someone yelled at Malloy, "Won't they be able to
jump their horses out of the boxcar, Dan?"

"Those Militia horses? Hell no! If one of them did
jump he'd likely break his leg."

Youngbear sat on the edge of the handcar, legs
dangling, staring moodily into the darkness. He was
thinking about Joe Chavez. He was wondering what the
sheriff would expect of him if he was alive.

He would, first of all, expect him to keep the peace
if that was humanly possible. Secondly, he would expect

him to bring Harvey TenEyck in to jail. Thirdly, he would expect him to find and arrest the man who had fired a shotgun blast point-blank into his chest earlier tonight.

Three things, none of them easy. The peace, he thought, would be kept until daylight. With the Militia out of it, TenEyck seemed, for the time being at least, to have the advantage. TenEyck had almost three times as many men as Ludlow did.

The handcar chugged into the Mesilla station and stopped beside the depot. TenEyck's voice called from the darkness, "Get it done, Dan?"

Dan Malloy jumped off the handcar onto the station platform. "Yes, sir. We blew that trestle ten miles north. Stopped the train all right."

Youngbear stepped off the handcar and without speaking to anyone went to where his horse was tied. He mounted and crossed the tracks, afterward angling toward the road that led to Crown. Behind him he heard King TenEyck bawl, "Deputy! Youngbear!" and when he got no answer, query plaintively, "Now where the hell do you suppose he went?"

Clear of town and across the bridge, he kicked his horse's sides and forced the animal into a steady lope. He had enough time to capture Harvey TenEyck and bring him back to town. But he didn't have any time to waste.

18.

As Youngbear rode swiftly toward Crown, he couldn't help thinking how much had happened in the last thirty hours. He thought of Joe Chavez, lying dead at Phinney's Funeral Parlor, and he felt a bleak sense of loss. It would be a long time before he could fully accept the fact that Chavez was gone. It would be longer before he stopped feeling so goddam lost.

Again he asked himself if this was what Joe Chavez would have done if he had lived. He came up with no really satisfactory answer. But it seemed to be the right thing to do, maybe the only thing that could be done to stop the bloodshed that would otherwise begin in Mesilla at dawn.

He passed the Jaramillo shack where all this trouble had begun. He could see it from the road, not clearly, but only as a darker blur against the dark land around it and beyond. He went on, and after he had passed through Crown's gate, quickly left the road, afterward paralleling it but riding a quarter mile away. He didn't want to meet any Crown employees who might happen to be heading toward town. He had no explanation they would accept as to why he was riding here.

Time dragged. He passed the town Rork and Governor Ludlow's State Police had burned. A wind was blowing toward him from it, and the smell of smoldering wood was strong. At one place, smoke was so thick he coughed.

He kept his horse at a steady lope, only slowing occasionally to let the horse blow. And at last he brought the towering house at Crown in sight.

He stopped and for several minutes sat still, watching the house and the buildings surrounding it. There was a light in an upstairs window of the house, another one downstairs. There was a light in the bunkhouse. Otherwise the place was dark.

As he watched, another light winked on in a small building that adjoined the bunkhouse. The cookshack, he supposed. The cook was already up, starting breakfast for the crew.

He would have to hurry or he might get back to town too late. But he didn't dare proceed recklessly. He knew that despite the fact that most of Crown was dark, there were sentries stationed around it, watching, guarding against the governor's men trying to slip in unseen and take Harvey prisoner, perhaps also to guard against Harvey slipping away.

He rode on at last, but a quarter mile from the house, he stopped again. There was a fence here, separating the hayfield from the surrounding range. He tied his horse to a fence post and stealthily followed the fenceline toward the house.

Every hundred feet or so he halted, studying the darkness ahead, listening for sounds. He got as close as two hundred yards before he saw the flare of a match ahead, and afterward the glow of a cigarette. Frowning, he waited, trying to pierce the darkness with his glance. A light smell of tobacco smoke came to him, and a rustling noise as the guard moved restlessly about.

Youngbear went on. He was half-Indian, he told himself, even if he hadn't been raised like one. He ought to be able to slip up on this unsuspecting guard without being seen or heard. The man was bored with standing guard. He was restless and tired and he was probably sleepy too. He wasn't expecting anything.

Step by careful step, Youngbear advanced. He would see the glow of the cigarette briefly and then it would disappear. He guessed from this that the guard was facing away from him, partially at least. He would see the cigarette as the sentry drew on it. It would disappear behind the bulk of his body as he lowered it in his hand.

Youngbear was now only fifteen feet away. He could hear the sound as the man exhaled the smoke, the smell of which was stronger now. He took a step, and another, and another still, testing the ground each time before putting his weight on it.

When he was only six feet away his foot snapped a twig. Then man started, and began to turn. Youngbear, lunging forward, hit him on the side of the head with a hard clenched fist.

Stunned, the man fell away, with Youngbear following like a mountain lion. He landed astraddle of the man's body, and struck twice more with his fists. One blow landed high on the man's cheekbone. The other struck him on the angle of the jaw.

The guard slumped, unconscious. Youngbear ripped away half of the man's shirtfront. Opening his mouth, he stuffed the cloth into it. He tore off another strip and tied the gag in place.

Now he yanked the man's belt out of the loops in his pants. He bound his hands behind him with the belt, hoping he got it tight enough but not so tight it cut the circulation off entirely. Finished with that, he took the man's cartridge belt from around his waist and bound his ankles together with it.

He didn't know how long the man would remain unconscious. Not more than five or ten minutes at the most. But with luck, that would be enough.

He moved forward swiftly now, running in a low crouch straight toward the house. He felt justified in assuming that he would encounter no more guards before he reached it. TenEyck would have surrounded the house with guards, probably fifty or a hundred yards apart. He would have more guards inside the house itself, but in between it should be clear.

Youngbear reached the wall of the house and stopped in its shadow, waiting for his harsh and rapid breathing to grow quiet again. Meanwhile, he searched the darkness carefully with his glance. He saw no movement, heard no unusual sounds. There must be dogs on the place, he thought, and hoped fervently he could avoid being discovered by them a few minutes more. If the dogs discovered him and began to bark, he'd have no alternative but to rush the house and try to get to Harvey before the remaining guards got to him.

His breathing normal once more, he edged along the wall. He was fairly familiar with this place, having been here many times in the past. He reached the porch and vaulted lightly over the rail, coming down with a soft, faint thump. He made that noise deliberately. He wanted to draw the inside guards out onto the porch.

He flattened himself beside the door. He heard steps inside the house and heard a man ask irritably, "Now what the hell was that?"

The door opened, throwing a rectangle of light on the floor of the porch. The screen door was pushed open and a man peered out.

Youngbear hit him solidly on the back of the neck with a clenched fist brought down like a sledge. The man pitched forward to lie face down on the floor before the door.

Youngbear knew this one would be unconscious for a long time. There was no need to tie him up. He stepped over the man's body into the big living room of the house. A startled mongrel leaped at him, teeth bared, a growl starting in his throat.

Youngbear stood his ground and when the dog was in range, kicked out savagely. His boot caught the dog in the throat and he yelped with pain. Youngbear said harshly, "Shut up, you son-of-a-bitch."

The dog, head down and tail between his legs, slunk away. Youngbear saw no other guards. He crossed the room, hurrying, and took the stair-steps three at a time. At the head of the stairs, he glanced both ways along the hall. Light came from beneath a door partway down the hall. He hurried to it and opened it.

Harvey was asleep on the bed, fully dressed. There was a bottle overturned on the floor beside the bed and the room reeked of whiskey fumes.

Youngbear cursed disgustedly under his breath. He crossed the room and shook Harvey angrily. "Come on, goddam it, come alive! Hey! Wake up!"

Harvey groaned. Youngbear shook him again and Harvey cursed protestingly. Youngbear released him and crossed the room. On the washstand was a white china pitcher of water. He went back to the bed and poured it, deliberately and slowly, into Harvey's upturned face.

Harvey gasped and began to choke as water went into his nose and mouth. He opened his eyes and tried to roll over, but Youngbear grabbed him by the hair and held his head still.

Harvey began to fight, flailing out with his arms, kicking with his feet. He knocked the pitcher out of Youngbear's hands and it shattered on the floor.

Youngbear, thoroughly angered, yanked Harvey into a sitting position on the edge of the bed. He slapped him, hard, first on one side of his face, then on the other. Harvey glared at him. Youngbear stepped back and Harvey got to his feet. He swung at Youngbear, but the deputy avoided the blow easily. Stepping in close, he slapped Harvey's face again.

Harvey was thoroughly enraged by now and his fury seemed to sober him. He yelled, "You red Indian son-of-a-bitch! I'll kill you!"

Youngbear grinned. "Sure. Come on. Kill me like you killed Mary Ludlow."

"God damn you . . . !"

Youngbear took the handcuffs from his pocket. He cuffed Harvey's right wrist to his own left one. Gun in hand and dragging a staggering Harvey TenEyck, he headed for the door.

The dog waiting at the bottom of the stairs, looking up, his tail wagging tentatively. Youngbear said harshly, "Go lie down, damn you! Get out of the way!"

The dog's tail stopped wagging and he slunk away. Youngbear dragged Harvey down the stairs. They crossed the living room to the door. The guard lay still unconscious on the porch the way Youngbear had left him.

Before going out, Youngbear said softly, "Open your mouth and I'll shut it with the barrel of this gun. Is that clear?"

"It's clear." Harvey's voice was sullen now, thick with liquor. He was unsteady but he wasn't drunk.

Youngbear headed away from the house toward the place he had left his horse. He and Harvey would just have to ride double. He didn't dare risk going to the corral for another horse.

It was impossible to be quiet with Harvey stumbling

along behind him. Even if Harvey didn't cry out, there was a good chance the guards would hear.

But they reached Youngbear's horse without incident. Uncuffing Harvey, Youngblood mounted. He gave Harvey the stirrup and Harvey mounted behind him. Harvey asked angrily, "What are you so goddam sore about?"

Youngbear kicked the horse into motion, heading back toward town. He said, more cruelly than he had intended, "I'll tell you why. You were too goddam gutless to blow your own brains out after you'd killed Mary, and because you were several men are dead and more are going to die."

Harvey's voice came subdued. "Who?"

"The sheriff's the latest one. Joe Chavez. And by God, for your information, he was worth fifty of the likes of you!"

Harvey was silent for a time. Then he asked, "Who else?"

"Three, out at that employees' town between here and Mesilla. And a couple of kids burned pretty bad."

"Oh Jesus!" Harvey breathed. After a moment of silence, he said, "I'm sorry, Jesse. I'm sorry, even if that doesn't do any good."

"You're right, it doesn't do any good."

"What are you going to do with me?"

"Put you in jail and hope to God that quiets the whole thing down."

"It won't, I know my pa."

"I doubt if you know him any better than he knows

you." He turned his head slightly, thinking he had heard a shout. He saw the lights go on in the house at Crown, upstairs and down, until the whole place was ablaze with light. He said sourly, "Well, one or both of the guards I slugged must have come to."

"You'll never get to town. They'll catch you and . . ."

"And what? Shoot me? I doubt that. If they do start shooting, you're the one that will get it first." He had professed to be unconcerned, but he was not. He kicked the overburdened horse into a lope.

Harvey asked, "Do you think I care?"

Youngbear said cruelly, "You care. You bungled your chance to convince anybody you didn't care."

He held the horse to a steady lope. The animal was strong and relatively fresh and he'd probably make it to town all right without giving out. Youngbear stayed well off the road, glancing behind often and listening carefully for sounds of pursuit.

He was almost to the gate when half a dozen men thundered past on the road, a quarter mile away. He halted his horse until they had gone by. Harvey made no attempt to yell or call out to them.

Youngbear cursed softly beneath his breath. Now TenEyck would be watching for him to arrive. His chance of getting into town unobserved was gone.

At least he thought TenEyck and his men wouldn't shoot at him. In darkness they'd be unable to without taking a chance of hitting Harvey too.

But there'd be nothing to keep Ludlow and his State Police from blazing away at both of them. Or would there? Didn't Ludlow want more than to see Harvey shot down in the street?

Maybe, he told himself, he'd make it after all. But if he thought he would, why was that core of ice spreading through his chest?"

19.

Streaks of gray touched the eastern sky as Youngbear and Harvey rode past the Jaramillo shack. Harvey wouldn't look at it. He kept his face turned in the opposite direction. Youngbear could feel the way his body stiffened, but he didn't say anything.

By the time they reached the bridge, the gray in the east was touched with rose, and by the time they reached the depot, it was light enough to see a block.

TenEyck's men were clustered around the depot. They moved out into the street as he approached, blocking it. Youngbear felt sorry for Harvey in spite of all the trouble he had caused. It was hard enough being TenEyck's son. It was harder being a coward, branded so before the whole population of the countryside. And a woman killer besides.

Youngbear stopped his horse and stared at the men blocking the street in front of him. He said, "Get out of the way. I'm going through."

Dan Malloy stepped forward. "That's up to us, Deputy. We can stop you if we want."

Youngbear glanced toward the Elkhorn Hotel. It was a little more than two blocks away, no more than two hundred yards. He could see men in all of the windows and he could see that all of them were armed. He said, "Look at the hotel, Malloy. If you try to take Harvey away from me Ludlow's men are going to cut loose on you."

Malloy looked doubtful. Turning his head he asked one of his men, "Where did Mr. TenEyck go?"

The voice of King TenEyck answered him from the depot platform. "I'm here."

"What do you want us to do, Mr. TenEyck? Should we let them through?"

TenEyck strode to the edge of the platform. He looked at Youngbear. He ignored his son entirely. "How do you know Ludlow's men won't kill you both when you ride past?"

"Ludlow knows by now that something happened to the train. He knows his Militia aren't coming right away. So I don't figure he's going to do anything that will make you any more anxious to attack the hotel than you already are."

"Hell, Ludlow isn't rational."

"He's as rational as you are."

TenEyck was silent a moment, frowning. At last he asked, "Why do you have to take Harvey to jail this way? Couldn't you go around?"

"Sure. But this way, Ludlow will see me taking Harvey

to jail. He won't be able to claim that justice isn't being done."

TenEyck thought that over a moment. He still had not looked directly at his son. At last he nodded. "All right. Go ahead."

Behind Youngbear, Harvey suddenly shouted, "Now wait a minute! Wait a goddam minute! Don't I have anything to say about all this?"

TenEyck looked at him. There was distaste in his expression that bordered on contempt. There was also puzzlement as though he had finally admitted to himself that he would never understand his son. He said, "You don't have anything to say."

The men made a passageway through their ranks and let Youngbear through. He rode slowly up Main Street toward the hotel. He looked up at each window in turn. He saw blue-uniformed State Police, each man armed with a rifle. He saw Sam Rork, battered and glowering. But he did not see the governor.

Drawing abreast, he finally saw Governor Ludlow step from the front door of the hotel. Up beyond, Daisy Kyle suddenly came from a side street and turned into Main. She was driving her buggy and he wondered fleetingly why she was in town so early. She never came to work until ten. Maybe she hadn't gone home at all.

Daisy was a complication he hadn't counted on. In a couple of minutes she would be directly across from the hotel. She would be in the line of fire if any of Ludlow's men cut loose.

He could see her face in the gray light of dawn. It was white and scared but she didn't stop and she did not turn back. He realized suddenly that she had planned this. She figured they wouldn't shoot at him if she was in the way.

He touched his heels to his horse's sides. The animal broke into a trot. And as though it was a signal, someone fired a rifle in a second-story window of the hotel.

The bullet missed cleanly. It struck the street and ricocheted, shattering a window in the Cowboy's Rest Saloon across the street.

Youngbear didn't even have time to dig heels into his horse's sides. He felt his revolver snatched from its holster. He heard the hammer cock and he felt the muzzle against his spine. Harvey said in a tense and frightened voice, "Don't do anything rash. Let's just stay right here."

Youngbear made himself go limp. He pushed his feet out well clear of the horse's sides. He said, "Don't be a fool. What's this going to get you? The minute Ludlow's men see that gun in your hand they're going to riddle both of us."

Harvey's voice, when it came again, was thin with fear. He said, "I'm going to take the gun out of your back, but I wouldn't advise you to try anything."

"Don't worry. I won't do a thing as long as you've got that gun." Even if he'd wanted to, there wasn't anything he could have done. His rifle was in the saddle boot and he couldn't get it out nearly fast enough to do any good with it.

Harvey yelled, "Governor! Governor Ludlow!"

Ludlow was already looking at him. Now he asked, "What?"

"Tell your men not to shoot any more! You know what will happen if they shoot us down! Pa's got more'n a hundred men down there."

"And if I do tell them that?"

"I'll do what I should have done night before last. That ought to satisfy everyone."

Youngbear turned his head. "Harvey, don't be a fool!"

Harvey didn't even seem to hear. He said, "Governor?"

Ludlow raised his voice. He bawled, "Hold your fire. Everyone!"

Youngbear wondered what he ought to do. He wondered what Chavez would have done in a spot like this. If he turned in the saddle and wrestled Harvey to the ground, Ludlow's men would riddle both of them. If he kicked the horse into a run, they'd do the same before he'd gone a dozen yards.

He guessed there wasn't anything much he *could* do. In the saddle behind him was a young man crazed with guilt and fear, a loaded gun in his hand. Up in the hotel were fifty of Ludlow's men, fingers on their triggers, hoping for an excuse to shoot.

He turned his head and looked at Harvey's face. It was a ghastly shade of gray. Harvey's eyes were wild. His mouth was compressed and trembling. The hand that held the gun was shaking violently.

Youngbear hardly dared to breathe. With fascination,

he watched Harvey raise the gun. The hammer was already back as Harvey put the gun against his ear. His mouth was working violently. He looked at Youngbear with terror-stricken eyes. "If I do this, will it stop? Will the killing stop?"

Youngbear said, "I don't know."

Down the street, King TenEyck roared, "Harvey! Damn it, put that gun down!"

Harvey's mouth firmed with decision at the sound. He squeezed the trigger and the gun roared, its sound muffled by the proximity of his head. Youngbear felt a fine spray against the side of his face that he knew was Harvey's blood. Harvey toppled from the saddle. Youngbear tried to hold him but it was no use. He hadn't the leverage and Harvey was too far gone.

Harvey's body hit the ground with an audible thud. Youngbear caught a glimpse of the governor's white, shocked face. Ludlow hadn't expected this. He was caught unawares and he didn't know what to do.

Youngbear dismounted. Down the street, King Ten-Eyck was already approaching, leading his horse. Up the street Daisy Kyle had hauled her buggy to a halt. Youngbear held her glance a moment, trying to reassure her that everything was going to be all right.

He wasn't sure in his own mind that it would. At this moment the street was utterly silent, but he knew he didn't dare let King TenEyck approach any closer. One hothead could turn this silent street into a battle-field. He stooped and gathered Harvey's body into his arms, startled by how light it was. Carefully he laid it across his saddle. Steadying it with one hand, the other holding his horse's bridle, he walked toward King Ten-Eyck farther down the street.

TenEyck met him at the intersection below the hotel. Youngbear didn't know what to say. TenEyck's face was stunned. His voice soft with shock, he asked, "Now why did he do that?"

Youngbear studied him. Surprised at his own temerity, he said, "Being a man was extra hard for him, but he finally made it. I think now you can be proud of him."

King TenEyck looked at him strangely. Frowning, he turned away and lifted the body of his son from Youngbear's saddle. His eyes were glazed and staring straight ahead as he turned and walked down the middle of the street toward the depot at its lower end.

Youngbear walked back up the street toward the hotel. He doubted, now, if TenEyck would go through with his attack. But even if he did not, there was work for the sheriff's deputy. Sam Rork had led men against the employees' town on Crown. He had burned it and as a result three men had died. Rork had to go to jail for that.

Another of the State Police had shot Joe Chavez and dumped his body behind the hotel. Senator Ingraham and whoever else had seen the sheriff shot had to be rescued from Ludlow's State Police.

He didn't look at Ludlow as he rode past the hotel. He went beyond and stopped beside Daisy Kyle's buggy. "What do you think you're doing here?"

Her face, which had been so white, flushed now with embarrassment. "I thought . . ." She stopped. Suddenly her eyes flashed warningly. "When I heard about the sheriff . . . Well, I knew you'd probably be stupid enough to try doing this all alone. And I was right. You could have been killed down there!"

"So could you."

"What are you going to do now?"

He said, "It's over. There's nothing more to worry about."

She stared at him suspiciously. He grinned. "Go put some coffee on. It's been a long night. I'll be right down."

Still suspicious, she tried to read his face. All he showed her was his steady grin. At last, with a little shrug, she clucked to her buggy horse and went on down the street toward the Cowboy's Rest.

Youngbear went on to the courthouse and hurried into the sheriff's office. His revolver still lay in the middle of the street in front of the hotel where Harvey TenEyck had dropped it after he'd shot himself. Someone would pick it up and return it to him, Youngbear thought.

He took a double-barrel ten-gauge down from the rack and broke the action. He stuffed in two ten-gauge shells loaded with buck. He put a handful of the same shells into his pocket.

There was a back door to the sheriff's office, one that was seldom used because it only led to a courthouse corridor. He used it now and continued down the corridor to the back door of the courthouse, which led to an expanse of lawn behind the building and out of sight of the hotel.

Hurrying, he crossed the lawn and entered the alley dividing the block beyond. They wouldn't be expecting him. His horse was tied in front of the courthouse and they would assume he was still inside.

He wasn't sure he could pull this off. His stomach was knotted and his hands were trembling.

But he knew he had to try. He owed it to Joe Chavez. And he owed it to himself. When he'd pinned on the deputy's star, he'd committed himself to whatever the job entailed. This was part of it. Only by arresting Rork could he satisfy King TenEyck and prevent him from taking the law into his own hands. Only by finding and arresting the killer of Joe Chavez could he repay the doubt he had owed the man.

20.

The sun poked itself above the horizon in the east as Youngbear reached the rear door of the Elkhorn Hotel. Across the alley he could see the place where Joe Chavez had lain, where they had dumped him like something used up and useless, like so much garbage or trash.

His chest still felt tight and jumpy but anger had heated his thoughts and driven the tremors from his hands. He hoped the back door of the hotel wasn't locked. If it was he'd have to blow the lock with his shotgun and that would bring every man in the hotel running to the alley door.

He tried the knob. It turned but the door didn't open. He gave it a yank and it yielded so suddenly that he staggered back. He recovered and stepped inside.

He was in a small vestibule off the kitchen. On one side were several big garbage cans. On the other were stacked-up supplies.

There was light in the kitchen. He cracked the door and peered through. A man was standing in the middle of the room, his back to the alley door. Youngbear stepped quickly in and, reversing the shotgun, struck the guard on the back of the head with its butt. The man collapsed.

There had been a clumsy attempt to clean up Joe Chavez's blood, but there still was a visible stain on the white tile floor. The bucket of mop water was a dirty red.

This, then, was where Joe Chavez had died. But what had he been doing in the kitchen? Why had be been shot in here?

Youngbear glanced around at the walls. Chavez had been killed by a shotgun and the range had not been close enough to absorb the entire charge. There should be a few pellets in the walls but he saw none.

A door on the far side of the kitchen opened onto a stairway leading to the second floor. Youngbear decided it was logical to assume that Chavez had not been shot in here at all. He must have been shot upstairs, must have rolled to the bottom, ending here.

Chavez had gone to the hotel to try and get Senator Ingraham away from the State Police. Ingraham had probably been in one of the rooms on the second floor so Chavez must have gone up this back stairway and at the top of it, ordered Ingraham's guards to drop their guns. One of them must have answered with a shotgun blast.

He crossed the kitchen and eased the door open, hoping it wouldn't squeak. It didn't and he went through, closing it carefully behind him. He started up the stairs, trying each step before putting his full weight on it. The shotgun was pointed up and both hammers were fully cocked. Youngbear could fire the barrels in quick succession. The resulting blast of buckshot, spreading, would kill everything in the upstairs hall.

There was a small window at the head of the stairs and there was a small light bulb burning on the ceiling of the second floor hall. Youngbear couldn't see along the length of the hall until he reached the second step from the top.

No guards were visible but light came from underneath the first door on his right. He tiptoed to it and listened. He could hear a man's voice but he could not make out his words.

This must be the room where they were holding Ingraham, he thought, or there would be no light. He didn't try the knob. Stepping back, he kicked savagely just beside the knob. The door slammed open with a crash and Youngbear, light on his feet as a bobcat, leaped through, the shotgun held ready at waist height.

Sitting on the bed against the wall were Senator Ingraham, Ronny Lort, the hotel clerk, and two Mexican scrubwomen who worked in the hotel. By the window were two uniformed members of the State Police. Youngbear said softly but convincingly, "Move and I'll cut you in two."

The two men stood awkwardly, as if frozen. One of them licked his lips. Without looking away from them, Youngbear asked, "Are you all right, Senator?"

"Yes. I'm all right."

"What are Ronny and those two women doing here?"

"They saw the sheriff killed. These men were going to wait until TenEyck attacked the hotel. We were all to be casualties of the fight."

"Which one of them killed Joe?"

"I didn't see it. The women did."

Youngbear, still without taking his eyes off the State Police, asked, "Which one of them killed the sheriff?"

One of the women spoke in heavily accented English. "Heem. The one weeth hees sombrero on."

Youngbear said, "Mister, you're under arrest, and I'll take your friend as an accessory. Turn around slow and face the wall. Don't try to shuck your guns just yet."

The two men hesitated. Youngbear said, "I don't really care. Joe Chavez was like a father to me. I'd as soon kill you as leave it to the courts. Make up your minds and do it fast."

The two looked at the gaping barrels of the ten-gauge in Youngbear's hands. Slowly they turned, their hands held carefully away from their bodies. Youngbear said, "Now shuck your guns."

The two guns were plucked carefully from their holsters and dropped to the floor. Youngbear said, "Hands behind you."

They put their hands behind them. Youngbear took the handcuffs from his pocket and clipped them to the men's right wrists. He said, "Senator, take Ronny and the two women and go down the back stairs. I'll be right behind you with these two."

Ingraham got up from the bed. He went out the open door. Ronny Lort followed him and the two terrified women followed him. Youngbear said, "All right, go ahead you two. But there had better not be any accidents like stumbling or bumping into things. The trigger pull on this thing is awful light."

White-faced, the two went out into the hall and down the stairs. Youngbear had picked up their guns and stuffed them into his belt while the senator, Ronny, and the two women were going out. The little procession now went through the kitchen and out into the alley. Youngbear handed the senator one of the guns. He gave Ronny the other one. "Take them to the jail and lock them up. I'll be there as soon as I can."

"What are you going to do?" asked Ingraham.

"Get Rork. He's the one that burned TenEyck's town."

Ronny and the senator herded the handcuffed pair up the alley toward the courthouse. Youngbear went back into the hotel. He'd been lucky so far but he couldn't expect his luck to last. Getting Rork was going to be a lot harder than getting the two who had been guarding the senator.

He felt strangely disappointed as he mounted the back stairs a second time. He realized he'd been hoping Chavez's killer would go for his gun. Ruefully he admitted that he'd wanted to blast the man with the shotgun the way he'd blasted Joe Chavez. He hadn't really wanted to arrest him and put him in jail.

He walked silently along the second-floor hall to the

stairs leading down to the lobby. It was crowded with
members of the State Police. Governor Ludlow sat on
one of the sofas with Sam Rork.

Youngbear was very conscious of the hallway at his
back. He knew there were men in each of the rooms that
faced the street. At the first gunshot they'd come
streaming out.

He started down the stairs, as quietly as he could. He
was almost halfway down before anyone noticed him.
A man yelled, "Hey! There's the sheriff's deputy!"

On the heels of the shout, a gun blasted. Youngbear
felt a blow like the kick of a mule against his thigh. He
slammed back against the stairs.

He recovered with an almost frantic effort, forcing
himself erect, forcing the shotgun level again, now
centering it on the sofa where Sam Rork sat with the
governor. He glanced involuntarily at his leg. Blood was
seeping through his pants. It didn't hurt yet, but the
sight of his own blood made him furious. He bawled,
"Goddam it, if anybody else shoots at me I'll let Rork
and the governor have both barrels!"

Ludlow's voice came high and thin, filled with terror
and the fear of death. "Hold it! Hold your fire! He
means what he says!"

Youngbear heard doors opening behind him, heard
running feet in the upstairs hall. Without turning
his head, he said, "Come on down past me, one by one.
Just remember that even if you shoot me in the
back, I'll be able to pull this trigger and kill Rork and the
governor."

Nothing happened. Youngbear said, "Tell them, Governor. You've got about ten seconds before I shoot."

Ludlow shrilled, "Do what he says! Don't anybody do anything except what he says! Do you understand?"

Youngbear heard the steps of a man starting to descend. He didn't take his glance from Ludlow and Rork as the man came past. Rork was livid with fury but he didn't say anything.

The second man came past. So did the third, the fourth, the fifth. Youngbear asked, "Is that all of them?"

Ludlow nodded, but his eyes gave him away. His glance went beyond Youngbear to the head of the stairs. Youngbear said, "You lying son-of-a-bitch! I ought to . . ."

Ludlow fairly screeched, "All right! All right! Come on down, Donovan!"

Donovan came past Youngbear. When he reached the bottom, Youngbear said, "One by one, I want you to come to the foot of the stairs and drop your guns."

Nobody moved. He realized they were waiting— until he would collapse from weakness, from loss of blood. He roared, "Move! If you think I won't kill Rork and the governor, just drag your feet a little more!"

They all moved at once, heading for the foot of the stairs. Guns thudded against the white-tiled lobby floor. Having disarmed themselves, the members of the State Police went to the far wall, almost out of the shotgun's deadly range, and formed a confused and irresolute group.

Youngbear knew that now was the test. He had to get down to the foot of the stairs. He had to walk far enough to take Ludlow and Rork to jail. If he faltered or fell down, he was finished. They'd kill him as quickly as they'd swat a fly.

Using the stair-rail, he pulled himself erect. Pain now washed over him in waves. His head reeled and spots danced before his eyes.

Rork was grinning triumphantly. Youngbear gritted his teeth but it didn't do any good.

Suddenly the door leading from the lobby to the street opened. Daisy Kyle came through, accompanied by Dan Malloy, foreman out at Crown. Daisy looked at Youngbear and spoke to Malloy. "Help him."

Malloy crossed the lobby and climbed the stairs. Youngbear said, "Take this shotgun and put it on Ludlow and Rork. I want them both in jail."

Malloy took the shotgun. He started to help Young-bear, but the deputy said sharply, "No. They're waiting for you to make a mistake. You get Rork and the governor. Daisy can help me all right."

Malloy went to the foot of the stairs. Daisy crossed the lobby and climbed the stairs to Youngbear. He said, "Help me up."

She did and the two of them went painfully down the stairs. Youngbear's face was bathed with sweat. He said, "Now help me to the door."

They made it to the door. Here, Jesse Youngbear stopped. He said, "Now, Malloy. Bring them out."

Malloy said, "Rork. Governor. Easy now. Just walk over here and out into the street."

Ludlow spoke to Rork out of the side of his mouth. "Don't try being a hero. That shotgun can cut us both in two."

When they were outside in the street, when Dan Malloy was too, Youngbear spoke to the men huddled against the wall. "You heard the governor. Don't try being heroes. He's going to jail and so is Rork. Whether he goes alive or dead depends on you."

He let Daisy Kyle help him out into the street. The sun was well up in the sky and the street was washed with bright sunlight. The sky was cloudless and the air was warm. Youngbear said, "A little more, Daisy. A little more."

She took his weight and helped him up the street, following Rork, the governor, and Dan Malloy.

It wasn't finished yet, Youngbear thought. Not by a long shot. But the chances were good that Chavez's killer and his accomplice would be executed. Rork would go to prison. And the governor?

It was doubtful if he could be convicted of anything. But even if he was not, he was through as a political power in the state of Colorado. Best of all, his State Police would be disbanded by his successor. With the death of his power, theirs would also die.

Every step was torture. But Daisy was soft and warm against him and her eyes, looking up at him, were soft and filled with compassion. And with something else that made him feel about ten feet tall.